LIKE A HOLIDAY INN

A PORT WILLIS ROMANCE

LINDSAY HARREL

To El Roi, the God who sees

CHAPTER 1

*I*f Rebecca Trengrouse could do one thing —and one thing only—for the rest of her life, it would be this.

This right here.

She sealed the plastic container of buttercream frosting she'd just whipped up and stepped back from the three layers of cake cooling on the counter. Inhaled the scent of sugar and vanilla in the air. Pictured how her hands would take what was in her head and physically make it reality in just three days.

Once she added the frosting and custom sugar decorations she'd been slaving over the last few weeks, the Donaldson wedding cake would be perfection.

Yes, perfection—something that could only be achieved in the kitchen.

A door creaked behind her. "Becs, it smells amazing in here!"

Rebecca tossed a glance over her shoulder at her friend Ginny Applegate, one eyebrow lifted. "Of course it does. This is a bakery." Ginny's bakery, to be exact—the one with the drool-worthy commercial oven her friend had graciously allowed Rebecca to use.

"Good point." Her brown ponytail bouncing, Ginny moved her lithe frame across the tiled floor to the white quartz island. "I'm so excited to see the finished product."

"I'm excited to make it happen." That's how she'd spend her time the day before the wedding, since the day of, Rebecca would be busy making sure the actual wedding went off without a problem.

Yes, she was cake baker, innkeeper, hostess, and wedding coordinator all in one pint-sized, one-woman show.

And she absolutely couldn't afford for everything not to go smashingly well.

After a slow autumn—and that loan she had stupidly taken out for kitchen renovations a year and a half ago at Rebecca's, her self-titled bed and breakfast in Port Willis, England—she needed the massive payday the wedding party would bring in.

Even if it meant the week of Christmas was completely bonkers.

Which was fine. It's not like Rebecca had any

other plans. Dad wasn't in town anymore, after all. And Blake was up in London with his little family.

She was alone this Christmas.

Just the way she liked it.

And no, she wasn't in denial—thank you very much.

Ginny stuck her finger into the bowl Rebecca had used to mix the strawberry champagne frosting and placed it in her mouth, mmm-ing with pleasure. "When does the wedding party get here again?"

"The twentieth." Just two days from now. The wedding—which would be held in the B&B's back-yard—wouldn't take place until December twenty-second, but the whole wedding party and their families would be descending on Rebecca's B&B in advance so they could settle in and enjoy their time together.

Ginny took another swipe of frosting. "I never thought you'd be able to top my mascarpone cream, but this is to die for. One point to you."

Rebecca allowed the corner of her mouth to upturn at the reminder of the friendly competition they had going. "As you Americans are so fond of saying, I had to bring my A game after I tasted your orange curd last week."

"Well, you most definitely did. Your bride is going to freak out over how amazing this is. Not to mention how beautiful it'll be once it's all put together." Ginny shook her slightly pink finger at

Rebecca. "You've got talent, my friend. I still can't believe you never went to culinary school."

Rebecca blew her dishwater blonde bangs out of her face. "No need for school when you're raised with a spatula in your hand instead of a rattle."

Ginny snorted. "True. I had to sneak baking lessons from our cook because my parents didn't think it an acceptable pastime." The woman may have grown up in one of the wealthiest families in Boston, but you'd never know it to look at her with her casual jeans dusted with flour, zippered sweat-shirt, and purple Converse sneakers. And even though they'd started out as enemies of a sort, even Rebecca hadn't been able to resist the charms of the bubbly American who made everyone her friend. "I'm jealous. I loved school but it was a beast."

"Well, you clearly made the most of it." Rebecca gestured around the kitchen. Five years ago, Ginny had opened Once Upon a Time Bakery after selling the bookstore next door to her best friend and fellow American, Sophia Rose. "Your bakery is more popular than Trengrouse Bakery ever was."

Ginny's face twisted into a grimace, just as it did anytime Rebecca's now-defunct family bakery was mentioned. "Becs—"

Rebecca carried her supplies to the large stain-less-steel sink and started washing them, falling into the familiar routine. "Thanks again for letting me use your kitchen to bake the cake. Your oven is a dream."

"Anytime." Ginny sidled up to Rebecca. "Look, I know you've forgiven me over what happened to your family's bakery, but—"

"There's nothing to forgive." After all, while Rebecca may have believed so initially, it wasn't Ginny's fault that Dad had decided to close up shop without even checking whether Rebecca wanted to continue the family legacy. He'd just assumed she didn't want it.

And why not? Rebecca had stayed away from Port Willis ever since leaving town at eighteen to attend college in Edinburgh. To her family—to Blake, Dad, and Mum, God rest her soul—it must have seemed like that.

They'd had no idea that coming back here to the small village on the Cornish coast, running the bakery, had been her dream since she'd been a little girl.

Now, her dream was just to survive. To not utterly drown in the blood-red financials of the B&B. If she could only keep on top of repaying that loan …

But it was fine. It would be fine. Landing the Donaldson wedding was just the sort of miracle she'd been praying for—well, not actually praying, since God seemed to have forgotten her too.

Regardless, the wedding would help her dig out

of the hole in which she'd found herself. She'd get paid, and then she'd experience a reprieve.

Until the next bill came due.

But for now, it was something.

"I still feel bad."

Rebecca hip-checked Ginny. "That's because you're too nice. Just be a cheeky bird like me and choose not to care what anyone else thinks." She scrunched her nose and lifted her chin. "There's a reason everyone in town calls me the Ice Queen."

Laughing, Ginny shoved her hands into the soap bubbles and grabbed a dirty measuring bowl and scrub brush. "Aw, Becs, you forget I know your secret. You're secretly soft inside."

"You go ahead and keep thinking that. You're the only one who does." She glanced around the kitchen, sighed. "If I could hole away here forever and never interact with another soul—save you, maybe—I could die a happy woman."

After a beat of silence came Ginny's teasing reply. "For someone who dislikes the human population as much as you do, it's a bit ironic you purchased a bed and breakfast."

Rebecca shrugged. It had seemed like a good idea at the time. Because if she couldn't have her own bakery, at least she could cook and bake for an appreciative audience in some way.

It had also allowed her to stay in her hometown, take care of Dad in his old age.

Though that hadn't exactly worked out the way she'd imagined it, now had it?

"Why do you think I put the blasted thing up for sale six months ago?" It had nothing to do with Dad's remarriage and move to Falmouth to be near Melanie's family.

None.

Okay, maybe a little. That, and the fact she was hardly keeping things afloat. And yet …

She plunged a mixing bowl into the suds and scrubbed. Hard.

Ginny paused, glanced sideways at Rebecca. "Still no offers?"

"No good ones." Everyone wanted to undercut her price—by a significant amount. It wasn't her fault the economy had taken a dip, that realty prices had fallen.

If she was going to divest herself of her livelihood, her home, then she was going to get a good price for it. Enough to start over.

To get a new dream.

Otherwise, her inheritance—the only thing her dad had ever given her—would be wasted. Gone.

With nothing to show for it.

"I don't understand how you haven't been able to find a buyer. Who wouldn't want to move to this gorgeous town?"

Now it was Rebecca's turn to snort. "It's tiny, for one. And sure, we have a few festivals like any small town, but as far as tourists go … well, the B&B sits below half capacity much of the time these days." Far below.

She lifted the clean mixing bowl out of the sink and snagged a towel to dry it.

"Surely you could find a way to drive more traffic in, yeah?" Ginny flipped her ponytail over her shoulder. "I know how you feel about marketing, but you're the only inn in town—"

"Don't you dare say that dirty M word to me, Ginny Rose." Rebecca shuddered at the thought of willingly putting her private affairs out there for the world to see. And yet, that was how most businesses worked, wasn't it?

It was official. She was, quite possibly, the worst businesswoman in England. Maybe in the whole world.

Ginny rolled her eyes, grinning. "Well, if you ever want some social media tips, or an updated website, you know Steven would be happy to help."

"Tell your delightful husband thanks, but no thanks."

"Alright, alright." Ginny held up her soapy hands in surrender. "But for the record, I hate the idea of you not living next door. I'll miss you so much whenever you go—though you know I'll do my best to convince you to stay in town even after you've sold."

Ginny was sweet, but her life had gotten so busy

after the whirlwind adoption of their three kids—four-year-old Macy and seven-year-old twins Lila and Jessie—that she hadn't had as much time to knock about with Rebecca lately anyway.

Between Ginny, her sister Sarah, and Sophia, who had a handsome professor husband and three kids of her own, most of the thirty-something women in this tiny village were living the wife and mom life. Something Rebecca would never have.

Because getting married meant opening your life to someone, and for Rebecca, that had only ever led to a broken heart.

She was better on her own.

"There's nothing left for me here."

"Thanks a lot."

"You know what I mean."

"I know you mean your family left. But I consider you family, Becs."

Unshed tears scorched Rebecca's eyes. Oh, no way. She was not going to cry. Especially not in front of someone else. That wasn't Rebecca's style.

"And speaking of that, did you decide about Christmas Eve?" Ginny continued. "And of course Christmas Day too. Or are you getting together with your dad and stepmom? Will your brother be in town this year? I keep forgetting to ask if he decided to come down from London."

Ugh. Could she bury herself under a pile of muffins and just avoid the holidays altogether? "I don't know what Dad is doing." And maybe she would, if she'd answered his calls or listened to his voicemails. "As for Blake, you know we're more of the *I'll text you on holidays and for family emergencies but that's it* sibling variety."

Sometimes she wished …

But it didn't matter what she wished. This is what was. First, she'd left. Then, she'd returned—and everyone else had left *her*. Apparently, that's what Trengrouses did.

"I'll be fine on my own." Rebecca forced a tiny smile. "There will be a lot of cleanup after the wedding party leaves. Thanks for the invitation, though."

"Well, it stands." Her friend chewed her bottom lip, looked like she wanted to say more. Of course she did. She wanted everyone to be as happy as she was. She'd invite a peddler off the street if she thought he didn't have somewhere to go for Christmas. Why not the Ice Queen too?

But that's just who Ginny Applegate was. Why the woman bothered being Rebecca's friend at all was a complete and utter mystery.

Side by side, she and Ginny worked until all the dishes were clean. At one point, Charlotte—the twenty-something, quiet brunette who worked the front of the bakery most days—stuck her head in and asked Ginny to come answer a question about ingredients for a customer. Ginny dried her hands and scampered off.

Rebecca turned to examine the wedding cake layers. Finding them completely cooled, she whipped up some simple syrup and brushed the layers with it to keep the cake moist. Then she wrapped them up and cleared a spot in Ginny's walk-in fridge for the cake. Her friend had much more space than she did and once again had showcased her generosity by allowing Rebecca to store the cake there.

Rebecca had worked up a bit of a sweat putting everything back where it belonged when she heard the door swing open. "I'm about done in here"—she glanced up—"oh."

Ginny had her sister with her. "Look who I found."

Though only slightly taller than Rebecca, confident redheaded Sarah Bentley-Hammett was the picture of poise—the complete opposite of Ginny in many ways, though they had the same smile. Like Ginny, Rebecca and Sarah hadn't gotten off on the best of feet, but they maintained a cordial acquaintance now. "Hey, Rebecca."

"Hullo."

"Need help with anything in here?" Sarah rubbed her hands together. "I'm on a break." She was an attorney and the president of the London branch of New Dawn Women's Council, a nonprofit that provided free legal aid to battered women. She and her photographer husband Michael had recently moved from Boston to Port Willis, his hometown, and she worked remotely—usually from Ginny's bakery—while he watched their toddler Judah at home in between photo shoots.

"You sure you aren't just avoiding a phone call from one of your donors?" Ginny teased.

"Ugh, fine. Yes." Sarah slumped against the counter. "He's such a complainer. I can't take it. My ears bleed every time I have to talk with him."

"Ooo, the old guy who thinks he's God's gift to all mankind?" Ginny threw her arm around her sister's shoulders. "Which is ridiculous, because we all know that's chocolate and peanut butter."

Sarah laughed. "That's the one."

A strange burning filled Rebecca's chest as she turned from their sisterly banter. She and Blake had never had that kind of relationship, though she was only a few years older. From what Ginny had said, she and Sarah—and their middle brother, who still lived in Boston and worked for one of their dad's many companies—hadn't been close until recently. The brother still had never visited Port Willis, but they talked via phone as much as he was able.

Sarah straightened. "I know I'm not a fabulous baker like either of you, but please save me from myself and give me a job."

"I'll leave that up to Ginny. I've gotta run."

Rebecca eyed the four platters of brownies and muffins she and Ginny had made this morning before she'd baked the cake. Time to get those stored in the B&B's freezer for later this week. Wedding guests tended to snack often in between festivities, and she needed to be on the top of her game.

Because happy brides spread the word. And weddings paid a lot—they not only booked out the ten-room B&B to capacity, but they also used the grounds out back for the ceremony and usually hired Rebecca to cater or provide the cake.

Enough weddings, and maybe she'd pay off that stinking loan.

Maybe she didn't have to sell.

Though sometimes, the idea of letting go of the inn felt right too.

Perhaps that was merely the exhaustion talking.

"Here, let us help." Before Rebecca could protest, Ginny grabbed two platters and Sarah snagged another, leaving one for Rebecca.

"Alright." Rebecca picked up the remaining platter, catching a whiff of cocoa despite the plastic wrap covering the chocolate cherry muffins, and headed out the kitchen door into the front of the bakery filled with tittering customers. With pops of yellow, Ginny's place displayed all the bright character and charm of the woman herself, inviting with its modern yet comfortable aesthetic.

Trengrouse Bakery had had history.

But Once Upon a Time Bakery had heart. Rebecca wouldn't have wanted to compete with that even if her dad *had* left her the bakery instead of retiring and closing up shop.

A bearded man with gray-streaked brown hair and a long black trench coat opened the door as the women approached, letting in a boost of chill along with a three-legged dog.

"Oliver Lincoln!" Ginny exclaimed, her attention directed at the man. "I thought you guys weren't coming in for a few days."

"Aunt Mavis is having a minor procedure tomorrow and needed someone to cover the antique shop, so we came early."

"Oh, I hope she's okay," Sarah chimed in.

"Nothing to be concerned about. She'll be in and out the same day."

"I'm glad to hear that." Despite the platters of food, Ginny crouched next to the white dog and let him lick her cheek. "And Rascal! Oh, how I missed you. Where's your mama?"

"Joy's next door at the bookshop doing that jumping up and down thing she always does when first being reunited with Sophia." Oliver's eyes twinkled as they always did when speaking of his American—and very boisterous—wife.

It was rather disgusting, actually. The way all of these women had come across the pond and turned

Rebecca's male British counterparts' brains to complete rubbish …

Fine, it was adorable, but Rebecca would never in a million years admit it. "We've got to get these treats back to the B&B."

Oliver held out his free hand. "Can I assist you?"

"We've got it sorted."

He nodded and held the door wider so she could slip through. The other women expressed their gratitude.

Rebecca probably should as well. "Oliver?"

His eyebrow arched. "Yes?"

"If you're available, you and Joy are welcome to join us tomorrow night at the B&B."

Sarah and Ginny exclaimed their agreement over the Lincolns joining in for the caroling and dinner tradition they'd started last year. Oliver grinned. "We'll be there. Thanks, mates."

"Good." Without another word, Rebecca turned and trudged onward, not stopping to wait for Sarah and Ginny to follow. From their chatter, it sounded as if they might be another few minutes, but this platter was growing heavy.

The sun set early in December, and the moon cast a gentle glow on the cobblestone street and pavements lined with black iron lampposts. The pastels of the buildings themselves had been muted to darker tones, but even that couldn't dim the beauty of Rebecca's hometown. At the bottom of sloping High Street, the twinkling waters of the harbor reflected the stars, casting an ethereal kind of magic back into the air.

Oh, why had she spent so many years away from this place?

Rebecca breathed in the crisp air. It didn't snow much in Port Willis, and that was one thing she missed about Edinburgh—the only thing.

All the people, the crowds … Daniel—those things she never wanted to see again.

This place smacked of home.

And yet, she wasn't sure she really belonged.

Because if home was where your heart was, maybe she didn't belong anywhere. After all, half this town didn't think Rebecca Trengrouse *had* a heart. Or, at the very least, that it was iced over.

It didn't take long to reach the B&B's front door. Rebecca wrestled it open with one hand and propped it with a doorstop for Ginny and Sarah, who were still somewhere behind her.

Turning, she promptly gasped back a shriek at the sight of a man standing at the wooden reception desk. "Who … What?"

The man removed his beanie and ran a hand through his crop of thick brown hair. His dark chocolate eyes sparked with amusement. "Speechless in my presence, I see." His American accent grated against her ears. He peeled off his gloves and stuffed them into the pocket of his leather jacket—one that must have cost him more than a whole week's stay at her B&B. Did they actually make leather that fine? "Don't worry. I'm used to it."

Her brain took a moment to process what he was saying. "I'm sorry?"

"No need to apologize, Beautiful." And then, this stranger had the audacity to wink at her.

She got the sudden urge to take a muffin from this tray and shove it into his impeccably chiseled face. "You're daft if you think I was apologizing. I don't apologize. To anyone. Especially not an arrogant dolt like you."

Instead of scowling at her like Daniel used to when she'd turn to a rant, the man's grin widened. And something about *that* was even more irksome.

"And here I've heard so many wonderful things about Port Willis hospitality."

Wait, was he a guest? She didn't have any reservations last time she'd checked. Rebecca narrowed her eyes. "Who are you?"

"Benjamin?" A squeal erupted behind Rebecca as Ginny rushed inside, followed quickly by Sarah, whose bootheels clacked on the wood floors. Ginny dropped her platters on the top of the desk and flung herself into the man's arms.

Benjamin? This was Ginny and Sarah's brother from Boston? The one they'd sometimes described as a playboy and serial dater?

That definitely made sense.

Ginny released her brother's broad shoulders and turned to Sarah. "Did you know he was coming?"

"I'm just as surprised as you." With a gentle smile, Sarah stepped into Benjamin's arms, then smacked the back of his head like the big sister she was. "You should have said something."

"I wanted to surprise my favorite sister."

Without asking which sister that would be, Sarah and Ginny looked at each other and rolled their eyes, as if used to their brother's antics.

Rebecca, however, did not have any familial obligation to stay in this room any longer than necessary and put up with this rubbish. Grabbing one of Ginny's trays along with her own, she high-tailed it to the kitchen and dropped them onto the gray quartz countertop. On her way back to take the other two trays, all three of the Bentley siblings turned her way.

Too bad she had already been spotted, else she'd have scooted back inside until they'd left.

Ginny put a hand on Benjamin's upper arm. "Benjamin, this is Becs—Rebecca Trengrouse. She's the owner. Becs, this is my older brother, Benjamin."

"We've met," he said. And there was that ridiculous grin again—the one that made her want to crawl out of her skin. Hit something.

"Yes. Most pleasurable moment of my life." Oh, how she hoped he could hear the sarcasm in her tone, though he'd have to be completely barmy not to. "Don't let me keep you. I'm sure you all want to get back to whoever's house Benjamin is staying at and get on with your family business."

Ginny opened and shut her mouth. Sarah winced.

Benjamin just stood there grinning at her like she was the Queen Consort inviting him to tea.

"What did I miss?" Rebecca's hand landed on a hip.

"Well …" Ginny tugged on her hair and separated the ends in that nervous way she had. "We only have the two bedrooms."

Yes, and all three girls were crammed into one of them with a bunk and another single twin bed.

Hold on. Was Ginny saying what Rebecca thought she was? "What about you?" she asked Sarah.

Sarah scrunched her nose. "Kara and Warren are staying with us. In fact"—she lifted her hand, checking her smart watch—"I need to head to the airport now to get them." She kissed Benjamin on the cheek. "Let's catch up tonight after dinner, okay? Come over around eight for dessert?"

"Sounds great."

Sarah rushed out. That only left Ginny, who still stood there looking like she'd snatched the last biscuit from the jar. She looked around the B&B—the dining room with a table for twelve, the sidebar where Rebecca set out food every morning, and beyond, to the cozy living room and fireplace lined with bookshelves. "You've got space here, don't you?"

Of course she did. At least until the wedding party arrived in two days.

But was the little bit of money she'd make from Benjamin's stay enough to make up for the fact that she'd have to spend the night under the same roof as this dodgy messer? Serve him breakfast? Put up with his arrogant mug?

"What about your couch?" she asked. "He could sleep there."

"Have you seen him?" Ginny hooked her thumb back at her brother, who bounced his gaze between the two women, mischief in his eyes. "Dude wouldn't fit."

What little mind Rebecca had for finances warred with her emotions. "Well, you're going to have to suss it out, because I don't have space."

"Really, Becs?"

Ooo, was that an edge of annoyance in Ginny's voice? Ginny, who had probably never said a cross word to anyone in her life? Who, in truth, put up with more of Rebecca's foul moods than anyone else ever had without complaint?

Rebecca pinched the bridge of her nose between her thumb and forefinger. "Fine. He can stay. Only two nights, though. I won't have room as of the twentieth."

Ginny's smile took up her whole face and her embrace nearly smothered Rebecca. "Thank you! We'll figure something out for the rest of the time. Right, bro?" She looked back at Benjamin.

"Sure we will."

"Great. I've got to get back to the bakery." She pointed at her brother and then to Rebecca. "You two play nice." Then she was gone.

"I'll be nice. Perfectly nice." Benjamin stroked his stubbled jaw and winked at Rebecca. "Maybe by the time I have to leave, you won't want me to go." Then he reached into his pocket, pulled out his wallet, and held out his credit card to Rebecca.

She rounded the desk, yanked the card from his grip, stuck it in the card reader, and leaned forward to meet his overconfidence head-on. "And maybe a blizzard will hit Port Willis." Ha. If they even got a small dusting of snow each year—especially at Christmastime—they'd be lucky. Any significant snow the meteorologists ever forecasted always seemed to skip right over their little village.

The printer whirred as it printed his receipt. She snagged it and handed it to him, along with a biro.

He slanted closer as he took the ballpoint pen. "So you're saying it's a possibility then?"

Well, technically there had been that blizzard in 1891 that was famous in these parts. But that had been a freak storm. Never likely to be repeated again.

"Possible only if I fall and whack my head and forget I have a brain. Sure. There's a chance."

If she'd thought Benjamin's smile had been bright before, what he shot her now had her eyes burning. "A chance is all I need."

CHAPTER 2

There was nothing like the early morning hours, baking sock-footed in her kitchen, the oven spreading its warmth, the glow from the lamppost outside casting light through the frosted windowpanes.

It was her favorite time of day. Things were peaceful in this space.

Funny enough, it was in the peace, in the quiet, that she felt the loneliness the least. Because it wasn't a natural time to spend with loved ones, when much of the world was still in bed.

It was a time she didn't have to miss what she couldn't have.

What she hadn't had since she was eleven, when Nana—the only person who'd ever truly seen Rebecca—had died.

Humming "White Christmas," she lowered the

oven door and breathed in the scent of fresh-baked scones. Rebecca smiled. Golden, flaky, and perfect.

She stuck on an oven glove and reached inside to pull out the baking tray.

"That's one of my favorite Christmas songs."

Yelping at the sudden intrusion, she jolted and yanked the tray out, clipping her wrist on the hot coils on her way out. The tray clattered to the stovetop as Rebecca hissed and rushed to the sink.

Unfortunately, her intruder—a Henley- and jeans-clad Benjamin—stood in her path. Which, even more unfortunately, meant she ran right into his solid chest and inhaled that clean laundry scent that somehow smelled better on men's clothing than women's. That, plus a hint of cologne she didn't have time to decipher. Because, yes, her wrist was on fire.

His arms came up and around her. "Whoa, there. You okay?"

"Do I look okay?" Pushing away from him, she clutched her arm and shook off the tips of his fingers—and the jolts they left behind. Her wrist was no longer the only part of her body that felt burned. Which was absurd. She was not the kind of woman to feel attracted to jerks like him, who interrupted perfectly peaceful mornings.

When she cut to the sink, Rebecca flipped on the water and stuck her wrist under the cool stream. "What are you doing in here? Guests are supposed to stay out of the kitchen."

"There wasn't a sign."

"That's just how B&Bs work. I'm sure given your family's wealth, you've traveled quite extensively and know these things."

And *she* knew men like him—men who didn't think the rules applied to them.

The air around her grew tight, combustible, as he moved into the space beside Rebecca. He took one look at her arm and frowned. "That doesn't look good."

"I've had worse."

"Ah, a tough chick, eh?"

"Call me a *chick* again and you'll find yourself out on the street."

He chuckled and held up his hands. "Alright, alright. Tough woman. There. Happy?"

"Happy? You're still here. So no."

If she'd said something similar to her ex-fiancé, Daniel would have blown out an exasperated breath. But not Benjamin. His lip curled up, almost as if he enjoyed their banter.

Wait. Banter? Nooooo. This wasn't banter. The bants was equal to flirtation.

And she most definitely was not flirting with this guy. Was he handsome? Sure. But handsome men led to devastation. Come to think of it, men in general did.

Dad had, even if he hadn't meant to hurt her.

He just hadn't even considered her.

And Benjamin wasn't considering Rebecca either. From what she'd heard of him, this was a game. He'd flirt, and if she let herself flirt back—become a plaything—then she'd have nobody to blame but herself when he left.

Because they all left eventually.

She flicked the water off, carefully dried her wrist, and grimaced at the red skin. Still first-degree, but it was gonna hurt like the dickens for a little while. Pushing past Benjamin, she walked to the last cabinet and snatched out some antibiotic ointment and a sterile gauze bandage.

"Wow. You're prepared."

She turned and jumped to find Benjamin there. Apparently he didn't understand the concept of personal space. "This is not the first time this has happened."

"Ah. Hazards of the job, then?"

She needed to shut this guy down and get him out of there. Regain her peace. "Something like that." A pause. "You can wait in the dining room." Rebecca lifted her chin toward the door as she fumbled to open the ointment tube. "I'll bring out your breakfast once I've got this sorted."

Benjamin didn't say a word in response. Instead, he took the cream from her hands, unscrewed the lid, and squirted some of the medication onto his own fingertip.

She stiffened. "What are you doing?"

He lifted his eyebrows. "What does it look like?" Then, without warning, he gently took her hand and turned her forearm so the burn faced the ceiling.

She shouldn't let him do this, but she remained frozen in place, held her breath as Benjamin focused on the task at hand. His touch was surprisingly gentle—fairy soft—as he dotted the ointment onto the mottled skin. Then he reached for the bandage, unwrapped it, and placed it on the site. His tongue poked out the corner of his mouth, like a young child concentrating on his handwriting.

Her heartbeat increased. There was nothing particularly intimate about dressing a stranger's wounds—doctors did it all the time.

And yet, she couldn't breathe.

Couldn't remove her eyes from him.

He took her wrist in both of his hands and smoothed the edges of the bandage down with his thumbs. Then his eyes flicked upward, caught hers and held them there.

After a few moments of awkward pause, Rebecca blinked and pulled her hand back into her possession. "Th-thank you."

Yet another grin bloomed on Benjamin's face. "Now, was that so hard?"

"Yes."

Laughter erupted as Benjamin shook his head and bowed. "I do believe my evil plan is working."

Then he moved through the swinging door into the dining room.

For a moment, Rebecca could only slump against the counter. What in the world had happened to her in those few moments? Maybe Benjamin really *did* have an evil plan—one to prove he could get her to like him in the few days he was here. He had seemed pretty determined last night at check-in.

But she hadn't seen him again after that—mostly because she'd slipped off to her bedroom at the top of the stairs and hadn't left even when she knew he'd gone off to meet up with his sisters.

Shaking her head, Rebecca plated the scones, fried up some ham, and loaded them onto a serving platter along with bowls of berries and clotted cream. Then she moved out to the sidebar in the dining room, where Benjamin stood at the window staring out onto the street. "Here." She unloaded the items from the platter and turned to go.

He walked over. "You're not going to join me?"

She smoothed down her gray apron, which she wore over her standard black slacks and a black long-sleeved shirt. "I don't typically eat with the guests."

"Not even when there's only one? Come on. I'm going to feel lonely." He put on a pout that probably worked miracles on other women.

Not her. But she could see how others might find it mildly adorable. Possibly even sexy.

Pursing her lips, Rebecca crossed her arms over her chest. "From what I hear, you're rarely lonely, so one meal won't kill you."

Was it her imagination or did something inconstant flicker in his brown eyes? But no, he recovered his grin quickly. "Fine, don't eat. But at least tell me about that sign out front while I eat."

"What sign?" She moved to the window, where the barest edge of sunlight had begun to shimmer on the horizon. There, hanging on a wooden stake in the cold ground, her For Sale sign shook in the wind. "Oh." She faced him again. "I'm selling the inn."

Benjamin's hand froze mid-reach for a scone. "Really?" His voice stretched out the first syllable of the word. "For how much?"

She told him.

He laughed as he split a scone in half and plopped it onto his plate. "No, seriously. How much?"

"What makes you think I'm kidding?"

"Because that's much too high." After spooning cream and berries onto one half of his scone, he placed the other half on top. "Don't get me wrong, this is a beautiful property. So much history. But I couldn't help but notice a few ..."

"Go on. A few what, exactly?"

He glanced up at her, meeting her gaze and holding it. Benjamin Bentley most definitely was not afraid of her. And why should he be? He towered over her. If he was really the high-ranking business official his sisters said, he was used to battling powerful men and women in suits.

But what he didn't know was that Rebecca could be just as scary. And she didn't give up.

"Go on," she repeated through clenched teeth. "Continue with your slander of my lovely property."

"It's not slander. You know what I'm saying is true." He forked a piece of ham before taking a casual seat at the long wooden table. "I just notice that the place could use a little updating. The roof looks a bit patchy in places. The wood on the back porch is warped. A fresh coat of paint outside and inside would do wonders for the overall appeal. That's all. But it does seem to have good bones, I'll give you that. And a gorgeous renovated kitchen."

The kitchen *was* amazing. Double oven, quartz countertops, premium cabinets organized just so, a chef's fridge …

So *maybe* she should have allocated some of the renovation loan funds to repairing other parts of the B&B. But the kitchen was where she spent most of her time. Her happy place.

The rest of the building was fine, so why mess with it?

Rebecca pulled out the chair directly across from Benjamin and sat, elbows on the table, leaning as far forward as her short stature would allow. "It has amazing bones. You don't even know this area.

Who are you to comment on what's a fair price or not?"

"Actually, I privately invest in properties in addition to my responsibilities at Bentley & Co. And I've been looking for a property around here to invest in ever since my sisters both moved to Port Willis. Not sure how I missed yours."

"I'm selling it myself." Had fired her realtor before she'd ever listed it because the woman wanted to list it for less than Rebecca did. All she'd cared about was a payday. "Less messy that way."

"Less effective too."

"Yeah, well, I don't want to sell to just anyone." That wasn't necessarily true. But something in her didn't want Benjamin thinking she was incompetent. That she hadn't done much advertising of her sale because some part of her was clinging to the hope that she could find a way to keep the B&B. Or at least hold out until the economy recovered enough to give her a fair shake.

"Why not? Is this a family property or something?" He took a sip of water.

"Not that it's any of your business, but no. I bought it almost three years ago using money from my inheritance after my dad sold off recipes and equipment from our family bakery."

He set down his cup and studied her. Was he putting two and two together about who Rebecca was? Did he know she was the one who'd caused so much trouble for Ginny when she was first opening her bakery?

But why should she care if he did?

"And you're finding that owning a B&B is not to your liking?"

Despite the fact she didn't care what he thought of her—she *didn't*, not really—her breathing came a bit easier at the new direction of his questioning. Not the past, but the future. "If it were, would I be selling?"

"Who knows? Maybe you're having financial trouble. Got in over your head. Want to cut your losses and recover what little money you might be able to squeeze from what's left."

Her insides froze. Was she that easy to read, or was he just throwing wild guesses out there?

"The point is, I don't really know enough about you to say." With completely relaxed shoulders, he used a knife to cut through his ham. So civilized. So refined. Despite his playboy persona, he'd clearly been raised with a proper education. Probably even knew the names of all the forks and knives one might use at a fancy dinner party.

He didn't belong here. In this town. In this dining room. At this table.

With her of all people.

"Why are you here, anyway?" she finally asked.

"I'm here because I'm hungry and because, I'm told, this is a bed and breakfast." Then he finally took a bite of the ham and chewed appreciatively. Swallowed, satisfied.

"That's not what I mean and you know it." She paused. "Why are you in town?"

"Uh, because it's Christmas. And I missed my sisters." Benjamin shrugged. "Holidays should be spent with family," he murmured.

Maybe they should. But for some, that wasn't an option. "I'm guessing your parents weren't too happy about you coming here instead of staying in Boston."

"George and Mariah Bentley will never be happy about anything unless they're controlling everyone else." Benjamin's jaw took on a hardened edge. "But I'm done giving them the satisfaction where I'm concerned."

Darn it all. She wanted to ask more.

Wanted to.

But wouldn't. What was the point?

Thankfully, she didn't need to come up with a response, because Benjamin bit into his scone, and with that one action, his eyes rolled back in his head and he groaned. "Oh wow. Okay. That one bite was worth all the money I paid to stay here."

She couldn't help the flutter in her stomach—the one that always grew into a tornado when someone enjoyed the food she had made. Nana had called it evidence of a job well done, but it was more than that.

To Rebecca, it was lifeblood.

True purpose.

She may not know exactly what to do with her life after the inn sold, but this … this was a feeling she wanted to claim as hers forever.

When he caught her staring, she startled. Had he said something? "What?"

"You look a little far away."

"Just have a lot on my mind." Not that it was any of his business. She pushed away from the table and stood. "I need to prepare for dinner tonight. We're going to have quite the crowd."

When Ginny had first mentioned the idea of a quiet dinner after a bit of caroling, Rebecca had readily agreed—it wasn't often she got to cook non-breakfast food for people. But one invite had turned into many, and tonight, Rebecca's living room would be packed with a lot of guests.

She kind of wanted to hide already.

"Aye, aye, Captain." Benjamin saluted. "I'll stay out of your way, then."

She quirked an eyebrow. "You'd better." And she meant it. She didn't have the energy for his shenanigans. Tonight was going to be draining enough.

Oh well. She'd put on her happy face and do her best to have fun.

It'd be fine.

Maybe even … fun.

This was neither fun nor fine. Not in the slightest.

There were people—everywhere. Taking over the couch. Squeezed together on the cozy high-backed chairs in front of the fireplace. Playing a board game at the table. Running back and forth through the door leading to the back patio and yard with squeals and shouts.

The one shouting loudest was Benjamin as he chased his nieces around, pretending to be a "cookie monster" wanting to steal their treats. The man apparently knew how to charm children and adults alike.

Fifteen adults and ten children laughed, played, drank cocoa, and decorated the Christmas tree in the living room.

The sounds, the smells—popcorn and apple

cider, cinnamon—they reminded Rebecca of the holidays of her childhood. Back when Nana lived with them. When Mom was alive. When aunts and uncles and cousins from neighboring towns would all pile into the small Trengrouse home and bring warmth and laughter to the holiday season.

This was the same—but it wasn't her family.

Here, she was on the outside. An interloper.

Not that they treated her as such. As Rebecca weaved in and out of the crowd, her handy serving platter filled with gingerbread man biscuits and scones, each couple took time to chat with her. Sophia and William. Sarah and Michael. Ginny and Steven. Joy and Oliver.

And Kara and Warren, who lived in Boston—and with whom she couldn't help but feel a special connection. After all, they'd fallen in love right here two years ago in her B&B. She might have even pushed them toward each other in a few small ways.

She paused, watching them as Kara handed her nine-year-old daughter Rose a Santa and rocking horse ornament, speaking to her in low tones. Rose gripped it, stroked Santa's cheek, and looked up at her mom with something like wonder before turning and hanging it on the tree.

Beside them, Warren rocked six-month-old Tommy who sucked his thumb, content to sleep on his dad's shoulder despite the noise and Christmas music rumbling from someone's phone speaker.

Warren placed his free arm around Kara, who snuggled up against him.

The picture of family was so strong, it sucked the breath from Rebecca. She had no right to witness such an intimate moment. And yet, she couldn't tear her eyes away.

"Rebecca?"

She startled at her name and turned to find Charlotte Bermont along with Georgiana Davis and Luke St. Clair—all single locals who had wrangled an invite to this bash. Not surprising, considering Charlotte worked at Ginny's bakery, Luke worked at Sophia's bookstore, and Georgiana spent most of her time working as an event planner—but from a booth tucked away at Ginny's bakery. They were just a few of the strays that Ginny took so much pleasure in taking under her wing.

"Hi." Rebecca cleared her throat. "I hope you're all enjoying yourselves."

"Oh, we are." Charlotte's timid voice reminded Rebecca of a mouse. Of course, her towering height dimmed the effect somewhat. Charlotte pulled her cardigan tight around her chest. "Thank you so much for having us. My family isn't in town, so this has been … quite nice."

Georgiana and Luke nodded their agreement, even though their families lived in Port Willis. But so many of their school chums had moved away. Rebecca could relate.

But that didn't mean she had to be friends with them.

"Oh. Well. Of course." Rebecca held out the platter—which happened to make a nice barrier between her and them. "Anyone want a biscuit?"

Luke's eyes lit up. Despite his slightly crooked nose, he was a handsome guy with blond hair and a physique like an American footballer. Quite funny that his favorite thing to do was sit around and read books. "I'll take two."

At Rebecca's raised eyebrows, he grinned. "One's for Carter." His five-year-old son was here somewhere playing. Since Luke's mum lived in Port Willis, they'd moved here last year after his wife left so he could have some help raising Carter.

Georgiana—a raven-haired beauty who, despite the cold weather, was decked out in a skirt and heels —took one of the biscuits from him and bit into it. Groaned. "Smashing as always, Rebecca."

"Hey! You stole Carter's biscuit." Luke poked Georgiana's side.

She swallowed and patted the corner of her mouth with a napkin. "Correction. I stole your biscuit. Carter already has one." She pointed to the staircase, where a messy-faced little towhead finished off his biscuit and raced after Sophia's daughter Emily.

Luke's easy smile, directed at Georgiana, pulled at something in Rebecca's gut. From what Rebecca had observed, the two had become quite close—something like best friends—since Luke had moved back to town. She thought she remembered hearing that they'd even been mates as children.

Perhaps ...

No more matchmaking, Rebecca.

She straightened at the internal scolding in her head. Right. What was she thinking? She didn't care to get invested in these people's lives. Sure, it had turned out well enough with Warren and Kara, but these were not her people. They were just acquaintances. Town-mates. People she said hello to on the street.

She didn't need them to be any more than that.

"Well." Her chest tightened. "I hope you enjoy the rest of the evening." Then, before anyone else could say something to her, she raced for her refuge.

Once in the kitchen, she set her almost empty platter down on the island and leaned with both hands against the countertop. Breathe in, breathe out. Her tight chest eased.

But when she looked at her sink, the compression returned. Piles and piles of dishes stacked every which way. She hadn't had a chance to clean up from the cooking she'd done for dinner before everyone arrived. Before she'd served up some of the best Cornish hens and mushroom rice she'd ever made. Before the gang had forced her to go with them caroling in the bitter cold even though she'd planned to stay back and clean.

And now, she had an entire kitchen to scrub and get back into order before her wedding party arrived tomorrow.

But before she could move, the door swung open behind her. "Hiding out, are we?" came that baritone she'd come to loathe. Especially when it had belted "White Christmas" during caroling earlier this evening and its owner had kept turning to Rebecca with waggling eyebrows, as if they were actually sharing some kind of *moment*.

Now, in the present, Rebecca closed her eyes against the intrusion. Maybe if she imagined he wasn't there …

"You know that wishing me gone won't make me magically disappear, right?" Benjamin chuckled. Seriously. Didn't the man know when he wasn't wanted?

Or did the fact Rebecca despised him only make him want to annoy her more?

Her eyes flitted open and she glared at him as he moved to sit on one of the stools at the counter. Ugh, why did he have to be so handsome in his flannel layered shirt, down gilet, and fancy jeans? He cut much too fine a figure. Thankfully, his personality irritated Rebecca too much for her to ever find him truly attractive.

"Maybe I'm secretly a magician. You never know."

His pretty mouth quirked. "You're full of surprises, Becs."

"Don't call me that." Only Ginny and her kids were allowed. Not even Rebecca's family had pet names for her.

Except for Nana. To her, she'd been Becca Boo.

"How about Becky?"

She shot him a look that told him exactly what she thought of that name.

He laughed. "Reba? Bee? Beckaroo?"

Rebecca couldn't help but snort at that last one. "Don't you dare." She quickly hid her smile.

"Ah, she does have a sense of humor after all."

"Only when people are funny. And you most definitely aren't." She paused. "Benji."

"No." He placed his hand over his heart and pretended like she'd speared him. "Anything but that. That reminds me of that old movie about a dog."

"Don't think I've seen that one. Was it an annoying dog? One that nips at a person's heels and won't stop following them around? Because that would fit you quite perfectly."

"I'll have you know that Benji the dog is a hero. He's a lone buck who doesn't need anyone. But when people he loves are in trouble, he steps up and saves the day." Benjamin puffed out his chest and winked. "So maybe the name does fit after all."

She just shook her head, holding back a smile. Blimey. He was getting past her defenses. "Hmmm, I'll have to keep thinking then. Can't call you something that will make your head even bigger."

She stood and sashayed to the sink—half hoping he'd leave.

The other half of her ...

Ugh.

She stared at the sink. The tower of dishes seemed even more insurmountable up close. Nope. She just couldn't right now.

Rebecca sighed, turned, sank back against the counter. Rubbed her forehead. "To answer your original question, no, I'm not hiding. Not exactly. I have to clean up in here. And ... I just ... that's a lot out there. I'm used to living alone."

He swiveled on his stool to face her. "You run a B&B. Aren't there people around all the time?"

"You know what I mean."

"Well, I concede that my sisters and their friends are a bit loud and obnoxious, aren't they?"

"Their friends ... and their brother."

"Touché. I walked right into that one." He draped one arm along the counter behind him and tapped his fingers on the quartz. "I know I asked you this this morning, but do you actually like running a B&B?"

"I ..." Her mouth dropped open. She'd known him less than twenty-four hours, and already he was asking questions nobody else ever had. Sure, Ginny had teased her about the irony of someone like her owning a place where she had to regularly interact with strangers, but had she ever come right out and asked Rebecca if she enjoyed her job? Maybe because she owned her own business, and loved what she did, she assumed everyone else did too.

Rebecca swallowed. "I don't hate it."

"Not what I asked."

He was so bossy. "Well, even if I did hate it, I bought it. So, there's nothing for it now."

"Unless you sell it."

"Well … yes." But that didn't seem likely, did it? Not for the amount she needed.

"What would you do instead? If you could do anything?"

"I don't know." Not exactly. Because owning her own bakery was out of the question. Turned out she had a terrible mind for business. And the thought of leaving Port Willis, again …

She might not belong, but was there actually *anywhere* out there where she would?

"It doesn't matter. I'm stuck with this place in the meantime." Why was she wasting her time talking with Benjamin about this—even if he was quite easy to talk to? Maybe that was part of his evil plan as well. Rebecca squared her shoulders. "You wouldn't understand anyway. You've got the world at your fingertips." People with money always did.

"You'd be surprised." Something about his tone, low and throaty, sent shivers through her. And it niggled that desire once again—the one to snag a cup of cider, sit down with him, and dig into what he meant.

Dig into his story.

But that's not something she did. Not anymore.

"Well." She pushed herself off the counter and turned to the sink. "You should get back to the party. Your nieces are probably missing you." *And I don't want you here.*

"I will. It's just …"

She glanced back over her shoulder. "Just … what?"

"I had a thought. About your inn."

Turning, she folded her arms over her chest. "I'm listening."

"I want to buy it."

Her jaw dropped. "What? Why?"

"I told you. I've been looking for a place to invest in here for a while. I didn't tell my sisters because I didn't want to get their hopes up. Otherwise, I'm sure Ginny would have told me about your inn a long time ago."

Something in her gut tightened. "Are you planning to move here or something?"

"No." He glanced up at the ceiling briefly, then back at her. "I just like to be prepared."

"For what?"

"I don't know. Things."

So vague.

Ah. See? She wasn't the only one keeping things close to the chest, as it were. She was a fool if she thought this man was actually interested in knowing anything about her. He was just trying to butter her up to get what he wanted.

Her inn.

But she also would be a fool if she didn't hear him out. "What's your offer?"

He told her.

She shook her head. "That's too low."

"Come on, Beckaroo."

She narrowed her eyes at the nickname. "No, Benji-roo." Ha. Take that. Rebecca lifted her chin. "It's too low."

He got off the stool and advanced a few steps—not exactly towering over her, but she was tempted to take a step backward herself. Still, she stood her ground. She wasn't budging.

"My offer is more than fair."

It actually *was* the highest offer that she'd received—still not her asking price, but, along with the money the Donaldson wedding would bring in, it might leave her with a tiny bit of money to start over. To travel, at least. Maybe. She was terrible at math and would need to sit down and look at the numbers.

"I'll think about it."

"Good. Because I really like it here."

She shouldn't ask but … "What do you like about it?"

He took another step toward her. Now they were toe to toe. So close she more than caught the hints of the aquatic citrus scent he wore. She had to resist the urge to close her eyes again—this time not so he could disappear, but so she could better breathe him in.

She literally felt her knees weakening. Which was total rubbish for a woman in her mid-thirties.

"I like a lot of things." His eyes roamed her face. "I love the feel of this place. It's cozy. Inviting—despite the cold welcome I received." His smile teased. Her stomach swooped in response. "And it's romantic. The perfect place for people to fall in love."

Blimey.

He didn't mean her and him. That was … no. She loathed him and his arrogant, smug face. And if he was chatting her up, it meant nothing to him.

Thank goodness he was leaving the B&B tomorrow. She couldn't afford this type of distraction any longer.

"Becs—oh."

Benjamin casually stepped back and turned to face Ginny, who stood in the doorway glancing between them, a sly smile slipping onto her face. "What's up, Sis?"

"I didn't mean to interrupt …"

Rebecca tugged at her shirt and wiped her face of any expression—though she could only pray it wasn't red. Curse her pale skin and its dead give-away whenever she was embarrassed. "You're not."

"Mmm hmm." Ginny widened the door. "I thought you guys should see something outside."

Oh no. Was something wrong with the backyard? She'd hired a landscaper to ensure all was perfect for the outdoor wedding this week, but maybe something had gone awry.

Rebecca hurried past Benjamin, through the living room emptied of everyone but Sophia—who sat on the couch nursing baby Kathryn under a cover—and out the back door onto the patio.

"Whoa." Benjamin was right behind her, and she felt his warm breath on her ear.

But whoa, indeed.

It had started to snow.

She pressed through the crowd and extended her arm. Light flakes fell onto her bare hand, melting to water as soon as they touched her warm skin. She didn't remember snow being in the forecast, but winter weather here was notoriously dodgy and unreliable.

"This will make for a beautiful wedding." Standing beside her, Benjamin gazed across the grassy yard, where Scots pines, Aspens, and English oaks lined the hectare—the equivalent of about two and a half acres—of land. Many of her flowering bushes hibernated for the winter, but the bright crimson Camellias she'd planted a few years ago in honor of Nana—who had shared a name with the flowers—were in full bloom.

In the middle of the yard, not too far from the B&B, the wooden pagoda where the wedding ceremony would be held was already covered in loose, powdery snow.

Rebecca sighed—this time in pleasure. In peace. Surprising, given she was surrounded by so many people. "Yes." Her voice shook slightly. "If it sticks. Which it most likely won't."

"Don't be a Debbie Downer, Beckaroo."

She didn't like to be. But sometimes, she just simply couldn't seem to look at the positive side of life.

Maybe, though, for just a moment, she could put aside her fears, her doubts, and simply enjoy the sight in front of her. The squeals of delight.

Sarah and Michael took eighteen-month-old Judah out into the falling flakes and twirled with him in their arms. Steven had Macy on his shoulders and she opened her mouth to the sky, catching snowflakes on her tongue. Kara's daughter Rose spun in a circle with Ginny's twins, and Emily, Edward, and Carter chased each other up and through the pagoda while their parents looked on and laughed.

Nana had always said that snow changed things.

That it was like God whispering his love one flake at a time. That it had the power to do a miracle in even the coldest heart.

And snow plus Christmastime? Well, that had the most potential of all.

Rebecca didn't know if she believed all of that. But maybe she could feel a bit of thaw in her own chest here, as she looked on.

"The snow in Port Willis is something else," Benjamin said. "Think it could turn to a blizzard?" his teasing voice whispered for her ears only.

Her sharp gaze pulled upward to him and the crinkles around his eyes. This man … he was trouble.

Rebecca just shook her head. "As I said before. It's possible." She paused for emphasis. "But not at all likely."

And with that, she went back to her kitchen—to the reality of sky-high dirty dishes and a wedding party coming in tomorrow. A party that could make or break her business. It was her last chance to save the B&B on her own.

Because if she sold to Benjamin, if she let it go, then what would she have left? What would she do?

If she didn't have a job in Port Willis, where would she go?

CHAPTER 4

She couldn't remember the last time she'd slept so well.

Rebecca lay in her rumpled bed for a moment, staring at the ceiling. Her lips cold, she pulled one of Nana's quilts up and over her chin and blinked the sleep from her eyes. Yawned.

Five days until Christmas and there was so much to do, especially in the next seventy-two hours with the wedding party coming in today, the rehearsal, the wedding, the after party, and the cleanup once they left.

Her brain hurt just thinking about it.

She stretched and inhaled the crisp scent of early morning—then froze. What the …

The scent of acrid smoke clung to the air.

Fire.

Her B&B was on fire.

Rebecca leaped from her bed, threw open her door, and raced down the creaking stairs, looking wildly about for flames.

But wait. Now that her tired brain thought about it, it wasn't a fire she smelled. It was burning, yes. Just not like wood burning.

More like … food.

The kitchen. She ran through the dining room and threw the door open to find her one and only guest using a towel to fan puffs of gray smoke away from her cast iron skillet.

"Benjamin!" She advanced toward him, pushed him out of the way—which was not exactly easy, given his hulking size. There in the skillet, curled into little bits of char, lay what she assumed was once bacon. Rebecca turned on the extractor hood fan, then pivoted to the culprit. "What were you thinking?"

"You weren't up, so I thought I'd try making breakfast for you." He scratched behind his ear and had the decency to look chagrined. "You don't ever have anyone making you something."

Oh. Well. That was kind of … sweet.

But still. "Watch my lips as I say this to you. Do not ever—and I mean ever—touch my oven again."

He tossed the towel onto the counter. "You're cute when you're angry, you know that?"

"Benjamin," she growled.

Laughing, he held up his hands. "Alright, I won't touch your beloved oven again."

"There are scones over there, you know." She huffed as she grabbed an oven glove and took the skillet by hand, then moved to the rubbish bin to scrape the acrid remains of meat inside. The lid banged closed. "You could have just grabbed one of those."

"Thanks, Beckaroo." A pause. "Nice pajamas, by the way."

She glanced down and nearly groaned at the grinning dog faces on her old-person pants and matching button-up flannel shirt. They weren't fashionable but they were comfortable and warm. "Yes, well, I thought my house was on fire. No time to get dressed for the day."

"Is this your way of saying you were thinking of me when you got ready for bed last night?" He brushed his finger against one of the dog faces on her upper arm. Even through the thick fabric, she shivered at his touch.

She moved past him, to the other side of the island. "Yes, next thing you know, I'll be getting a dog and naming him Benji just so I can think of you all the time once you're gone. Which, I'll remind you, is today."

"That's a brilliant idea! Let's go dog shopping together."

Rebecca cocked her head and tried to muster a

glare. Either this guy didn't understand her snark, or he did … and it didn't bother him.

She didn't know which was worse.

"Hmmm." Rebecca tapped her chin as if actually considering his inane idea. "Sorry, can't. I have something kind of important happening today. Remember? Some of us can't gallivant around as if we don't have jobs."

"Ouch, Beckaroo. You wound me. It's called paid time off. Vacation." Benjamin moved toward the left-over scones she'd pointed out earlier and opened the poly bag, pulling out a savory pastry. "You should try it."

"What is this V word that you speak of?" He was so ridiculous. "Now get out of my kitchen."

"Do you treat all of your guests with such contempt?" Ignoring her directive, he moved to the fridge and stuck his head inside, rummaging around.

"Just the really annoying ones." She moved behind him and yanked back on his arm. Oof, it was solid. "Tell me what you're looking for and I'll find it."

"Got it." Grinning, he emerged with some golden syrup. Then, before she could exclaim over the crime about to be committed, he shut the fridge and spooned some onto the scone. Why would he use syrup when she had homemade jam?

She shook her head as he bit into the day-old

baked good, but when he sighed into it, Rebecca couldn't help smiling.

He glanced up and caught her. Darn it. His eyebrow arched. "What?"

"Nothing." She barked the word, hoping to scrub the memory of her smile from his brain. "Finish eating and then get packed up. I need to clean your room before my other guests arrive."

"But you're going to miss me, right? Just because I'll be gone from the B&B doesn't mean I won't be in town for a few more days." He took another pleasurable bite, chewed, swallowed. Licked syrup off of his thumb. "I'm not leaving until the day after Christmas."

"Good riddance, I say." She moved through the swinging door. If she stayed in there much longer, he was going to wear her down even more than he already had.

Because the truth? She was starting to not so much mind Ginny and Sarah's brother.

Maybe even … tolerate him. Like last night, when she'd actually *wanted* to talk with him, find out his story. When she'd been inexplicably drawn to him.

But Benjamin Bentley was a heartbreak waiting to happen.

And she didn't do heartbreak. Not anymore.

He followed her to the registration desk. "You sure you don't have room for me to stay too? Take pity on a good chap." He said this with a terrible

British accent. "Ginny and Steven's couch is teeny tiny. I might as well sleep on the floor."

"Might I suggest a lilo?" She wiggled her computer mouse, waited for her computer to kick on.

"A what?"

"I believe you Americans call them air mattresses."

"I don't think Ginny has one."

"It'll be the floor then, I guess."

He scoffed. "No compassion for my plight, I see. Just because you're cute and petite—"

She shot him a warning look.

"What? You are. And as such, you clearly don't have any sense of what it is to be a big, strong man."

Ho boy. Her lips twitched. "Neither do you."

"Beckaroo! You're killing me here." He leaned over the desk, into her space—just like he always seemed to do. Then he put on the most pathetic puppy dog eyes and pout she'd ever seen. "You sure you don't have some random space for me to stay?"

"You knew from the beginning that I didn't." She clicked on a random document on the screen, just to have something to do. "The only available room is my own—and you sure aren't staying in there."

"I wouldn't dream of asking that." He snatched a pen from her jar and clacked it against the wooden desktop. "Fine. You win. I'll go pack my things."

Her lungs deflated, almost as if she was disappointed he'd given up so easily—which was daft. Because of course he had to give up. She really *didn't* have a room for him to stay in. "Thank you."

Her mobile phone rang on the desk—she must have forgotten it down here on the charger last night after the guests had finally gone home. Rebecca glanced at the number to be sure it wasn't Dad calling again. She should probably see what he wanted, but not until after the wedding party left. She didn't have the emotional headspace to deal with family drama right now.

But no, it was Dora Donaldson. Rebecca used her mobile phone for private calls and for the B&B since she didn't want to be tied to the desk at all hours, and because she was the only employee—she couldn't afford to hire anyone else to man reception or do anything else around here. "Dora, hi." She turned her back to Benjamin, who for some reason hadn't yet gone upstairs to his room.

"Rebecca, so glad I caught you." Dora's voice sounded a bit garbled. "I'm terribly sorry to do this, but we need to postpone our arrival."

Rebecca stilled. "Oh? What's wrong?"

"I don't know if you've seen the weather but the snow yesterday put a lot of ice on the road between London and Port Willis. Travis just doesn't feel comfortable asking our parents and everyone else— myself included—to take the risk in driving down today."

"Of course." Her voice sounded as dry and stiff as her throat.

No, no, no. Rebecca did the math in her head as best as she could. Her cancelation policy had the Donaldson party paying twenty percent of the agreed-upon nightly fee—which Rebecca had already discounted as part of the wedding package. It wasn't nothing, but it also wasn't nearly what she'd been counting on.

Still, it was only one night of loss.

It was, right?

"When are you planning to arrive, then?" Ignoring Benjamin, who was very obviously listening but pretending not to—he was browsing the selection of brochures she kept affixed to the wall in front of the desk—she moved briskly to the front window and peered outside.

Most of the snow from yesterday had already melted, but the sky in the distance held legions of dark clouds. Were they due for even more snow to dump? Or would it skip over them as usual?

For her wedding party's sake, she sent up a prayer for melted snow and no more delays. Not that God really listened to her prayers. But it couldn't hurt to ask.

"Our goal is tomorrow morning. Afternoon at the absolute latest. We'll be watching the weather reports, but should be there in plenty of time for the rehearsal dinner."

Rebecca touched her fingers to the cold window. "All right. I'll see you tomorrow then. Keep me posted."

"I definitely will. Thank you, Rebecca."

Dora hung up and Rebecca stuck the phone into the pocket of her pajama pants.

"Sounds like I can stay another night."

"Eavesdropping is a crime in England, you know." She glanced back at Benjamin, who held three different pamphlets.

He laughed, then sobered. "I'm sorry your wedding canceled."

"They didn't. They're coming tomorrow." She straightened, marched back to the desk, and yanked the brochures from his hand. Reading the covers, she flipped them back around. "I didn't know you were interested in garden tea parties."

"Oh, but I am, love." There was that awful accent again. He mimed drinking from a teacup—pinky finger lifted.

"Uh huh." She flipped to the next brochure. "And surfing in the winter? If you're a beginner, I don't recommend it."

"I have surfed before, but it's been a while."

The last brochure featured a walking tour of Port Willis. She shook it at him. "And this? Really?"

"That one actually looks interesting."

"Yes, well, it's given by someone who hasn't lived here but a year. She moved down from the

Cotswolds and while she might know what the history books say, you can only really know the true history if you've lived here. Allowed the coastal air to seep into your bones as you grow. Listened at the knee of old-timers whose favorite pastime is telling tales of smugglers and shipwrecks."

Okay, oops. That speech had come from … well, she didn't know where.

"That settles it then." Benjamin took the brochures from her hand and tossed them into the small rubbish bin beside the desk. "You're giving me a tour."

"Me? No, no. I'm no tour guide."

"You're basically the perfect person."

She waved him off. "Ask your sisters to give you a tour."

"They haven't lived here that long. You said yourself—"

"Their husbands, then." She absolutely could not spend more time alone with this man. His proximity did strange things to her. She was supposed to be rid of him by now. And there was still so much to do. "I don't have time."

"Seems to me you have all day. And weren't we just talking about taking some time off to relax?"

"Being with *you* is anything but relaxing."

"I'm going to pretend you didn't just wound me terribly with that remark." He turned to walk up the stairs.

She placed her hands on her hips. "Where are you going?"

"To my room to change into something warm." He winked. "It looks cold outside, or didn't you notice?"

"I'm not giving you a tour." How many times did she have to repeat herself?

Benjamin moved back to her. "Okay, fine. We can hang out here then. What do you want to do?"

"I have to clean." Great. Did he hear the desperation in her voice?

"You had to clean my room today. That was all. And now you can't do that until tomorrow. Otherwise, you're ready for your wedding party to arrive, right?"

Grrr. He had her there. "You aren't going to drop this, are you?"

He stuck his hands into his pockets and grinned. "Nope. But if it helps, I'll pay you the one hundred pounds I would have paid Marissa What's-Her-Face for that Port Willis walking tour."

One hundred pounds? Seriously? For an hour of her time, maybe two, tops?

Rebecca shut her eyes. Couldn't believe she was about to agree to this. "Make it one hundred and fifteen and you've got yourself a deal."

"After the hustle and bustle of Boston, I can see why my sisters like it here." Benjamin and Rebecca leaned against a wooden railing on the edge of a bluff, looking down into the dark, swirling waters below. Behind them stood a park with a children's playground, a gazebo, and a Christmas tree the Grinch would despise. At night, its lights could be seen up and down High Street—even as far as the B&B.

"I'm sure it's quite small in comparison. We only have about one thousand residents in Port Willis proper."

Benjamin whistled and tucked his scarf down into his jacket. "It's so personal. Like that tree." He thumbed behind him at the behemoth, which was decked out from top to bottom with lights, silver garland, and ornaments. "None of the ornaments match. It's a complete hodgepodge of sophisticated and handmade, but somehow it works. Reminds me of trees I used to see in some of my friends' homes growing up."

"Not yours?"

"Nooooo. Mariah Bentley wouldn't put something a child made on her tree. Are you kidding? Not even if her life depended on it."

That was quite sad. Her own mother had relished pulling out the box of her and Blake's ever-growing collection of school project snowflakes, glittery popsicle stick trees, and colorful candy canes. The thought pierced and grated.

The holidays just weren't the same without Mum. Without Nana. Without all of them together.

Rebecca cleared her throat. She was here to give a tour of Port Willis, after all. "In the past, the parish council was in charge of decorations, so everything matched and glistened just perfectly. But last year, the village invited town members to contribute a meaningful ornament to the tree and this year it was cemented as a tradition." She and Ginny had purchased matching cake ornaments and had hung them last weekend during the Winter Walk—another somewhat new tradition that happened in conjunction with the tree lighting ceremony.

"Have they always put this tree up too?"

"I don't remember when they started. I'm not sure they did it when I was really young because I don't have any memories attached to it."

"Have you lived here your whole life?"

This tour wasn't supposed to get personal. But the question was innocent enough. "Born and raised. But I did spend fourteen years in Edinburgh."

"Oh yeah? What took you there?"

"Uni."

"What did you study? Business?"

"Started out that way, but I hated economics and accounting." Her brain just didn't work that way—as he'd see if he ever got a peek at the inn's books. She wiggled her hands inside her pockets. "So I dropped out. Got a job as a checkout operator at a grocery.

Applied to culinary school." Despite what she'd told Ginny, she'd have loved to gain a formal education in the art of baking.

"Just applied?"

"Yeah." She shrugged. "Come on." Turning, Rebecca started across the path that would hook back up with High Street and take them down toward the harbor. Wind whipped at the bottom of her jacket and blew her hair every which way. She should have tied it back, but had been much too flustered when getting ready—and absolutely *not* because she cared what Benjamin thought of her appearance.

Benjamin jogged to keep up. "You sure do walk quickly when you don't want to answer my questions."

"You didn't pay me to answer your questions, except as it regards Port Willis."

"This regards one of Port Willis's long-term residents. Seems relevant to me."

Without warning, she halted, turned toward him. "I didn't get in, okay? Wasn't good enough. That's the end of the story."

"No, it's not."

What was with this guy? "You don't know everything, Benjamin."

He reached out, cupped her elbow in his hand. The wicked smile he always sported had fled, and in its place was a frown. His forehead crinkled just under the edge of his blue knit cap. "You're right. I don't. But I do know that whoever made the decision not to admit you was crazy. Because you're amazing."

Her heart jumped at the tender tone. Almost as if he really believed what he was saying. "My food is amazing, you mean."

"That too."

Throat dry, she swallowed hard. "Yes, well. Amazing still wasn't good enough. I had to do an interview, and it just went terribly wrong."

They started walking again, this time heading down the steep street. A few midday shoppers were out, but the cold weather kept most inside.

"Don't tell me—you insulted the interviewer."

"No." Her answer was tight, quick.

He glanced sideways at her, eyebrows raised.

She sighed. "Fine. I may have had a comment or two about how he couldn't stop looking at my—" Rebecca paused, cheeks on fire. "Well, I told him where he could stick his dodgy gaze, is all."

Benjamin tossed back his head and laughed. "Aw, Beckaroo, to be a fly on that wall."

"Ha ha." She reached out and smacked his middle. Before Rebecca could pull back her hand, Benjamin grabbed it and held it hostage. She stared at their gloved hands wound together for a few moments before clearing her throat and tugging again. Harder.

He released his grip and stuffed his hands into

his coat pocket while they continued down the street. "So you quit college. What made you stay away from Port Willis?"

"It's complicated."

"Okay. What made you stay in Edinburgh, then? Work?"

"A man." Blimey. How was this guy getting her to talk so much about herself, especially in such a short time? Ginny had barely dragged her past out of her, and she'd had years to do it.

She sped up down the pavement.

"Innnnn-teresting."

"Not really." *Please drop it.*

"Oh no. It is. What—"

"I need to finish your tour." Rebecca started naming off the local shops, telling him about the owners. They passed the antique store, the inn, the bakery, and Rosebud Books while headed toward the harbor. Benjamin asked questions, and thankfully did not return to the subject of Daniel.

Then, before Rebecca knew it, they were in a place that was most familiar. Her breath caught and she stopped abruptly, nearly tripping Benjamin behind her. He might have said something to her, but her ears buzzed and her throat burned as she took in the darkened windows. The faded striped awning. She approached and set her trembling hand against the doorknob.

How many times had she gone through this

door? Pushed her way inside in the wee hours of the morning before school to help out in the kitchen in the back? Spent time with Nana, with Mum and Da, even Blake, tossing flour and kneading dough and laughing together?

"What's this place?"

He would ask that, because of course the old signage had been removed when Dad had shut it all down. The owner hadn't bothered re-leasing the place. She'd never found out why, but it didn't matter.

Trengrouse Bakery was only a memory now.

A fat tear rolled down Rebecca's cheek. "It's a tomb."

"Becs?" Benjamin's voice was soft now.

She clenched her teeth. "I told you not to call me that." Then she turned away from the memories and walked as quickly as her legs would carry her toward the harbor. This tour needed to be done. She needed to go back to her kitchen, to a place she alone controlled, her refuge away from the memories of the people who had left her.

Of what had been.

With his long legs, Benjamin kept pace with her. She wasn't much of a tour guide anymore, just walking, not talking, but he didn't ask her to.

When they arrived at the harbor, the wind blew even stronger. Boats thrashed in the now-roiling ocean and there wasn't a soul in sight. The storm was almost here. "We should go."

"What about that? Would you show it to me?"

Rebecca looked in the direction of his pointed finger. "The lighthouse?"

Hands still in his pockets, he shrugged. "I've always been a sucker for lighthouses. Ever since I was a kid. Kind of got obsessed, actually. My dad liked them too." He paused, managed a dry laugh. "Might be the only thing we've ever agreed on."

Rebecca opened her mouth to respond to that—but no. It was better to let things lie between them. To not grow this … whatever it was.

"Come on. Please?"

She gestured toward the sky. "I think more snow might be coming. We should head back."

"We'll make it quick. And we're both from strong stock. We can manage a little snow." He quirked a smile at her. Today his jaw was unshaven, and she caught the hint of a dimple beneath his scruff. "It's not that far, right?"

"Not if we hurry. But you should get your sisters to show it to you later this week."

He cocked his head. "I want *you* to show me."

Oh. She swallowed. "I—"

"Besides, I'm the customer. And isn't the customer always right?"

She couldn't help the smile that inched its way

onto her face—a welcome relief after the tears. "Do you really want me to answer that?"

"On second thought, no." He held out his hand. "Come on. Please?"

Why did tough Rebecca Trengrouse have such trouble saying no to this guy? He was a charmer. Not from her world. And yet, she didn't scare him away. In fact, it almost seemed as if he liked being around her.

As if he liked … her.

Which wasn't true. Couldn't be. Look at the man. Charismatic. Intelligent. Handsome. Rich. He could probably have any woman he wanted.

So why would he want short, mousy, uncouth Rebecca?

But he *was* paying her. She eyed the sky, then the lighthouse. "Let's climb quickly. It's a bit steep. Think you can keep up?"

"Challenge accepted."

A laugh burned for release in her chest, and she started to run up the grassy bluff that led to the lighthouse. He raced after her, easily catching and then passing her. Turning, he walked backward up the hill just in front of her, a smug look on his face.

"You're a rotter, you know."

"Believe me. I know." But this time his wasn't a teasing smile. It was a sad one.

And darn it, she couldn't help herself this time. "What do you m—"

That's when the snow began to fall. They were halfway up the hill when the flakes started to dot the landscape, their coats, their knit caps.

And it was coming down hard.

"Come on!" This time, when Benjamin reached for her hand, she took it. They ran together toward the lighthouse, heels kicking at the falling snow.

By the time they reached the old red door and ducked inside, Rebecca was out of breath and her cheeks were numb. Benjamin shut the door behind them and they both leaned back side by side, chests heaving.

"We made it." Not that it was much warmer in here, but at least it was dry.

"We did." Benjamin squeezed her hand.

She hadn't realized he still held it. Biting her lip, she gently pulled her hand back and pointed to the stone steps. "Want a better view?"

"You bet I do."

She led him up the steps, which the historical society did a decent job of maintaining despite their age. "They stopped using this lighthouse a long time ago, but it's a point of pride in our community. So much history." After a brief climb, they emerged onto a floor with a roundabout but enclosed view of the waves, the bluffs, the town below.

So much white already.

Something pinched Rebecca's insides. Hopefully the storm would end soon so the sun could emerge and melt all of this away before her guests arrived tomorrow.

"What a view." Benjamin removed his cap and ran his hand through his hair.

What would that hair feel like beneath her fingertips?

Rebecca pivoted away from him. What was wrong with her, prattling on—even internally—like a schoolgirl with a crush?

"This just might be the coolest lighthouse I've ever been to."

She couldn't help but glance over her shoulder at him. "Yeah?"

"Yeah." He just looked at her. No smile. Just eyes watching—taking her in. Almost like he saw her. Heard her inner struggles.

Rebecca shivered.

"Well, it has a lot of history." Then she plunged into all she'd learned about the lighthouse from the old men around the village. Benjamin moved his gaze to the ocean, watching the snow fall as she talked.

When she'd run out of things to say, he spoke instead. "I love that you have pride in where you're from."

Did she? Had that come across in her tone? "I suppose I do. You don't?"

He lifted his shoulders. "Boston's cool and all. Of course, lots of history there. But I don't know. I grew up in a town where everyone knew me not for who I was, but for whose son I was. My dad …"

"Ginny's told me some." About how their dad was a powerful businessman. How the Bentleys were richer than dirt. How their dad was also emotionally manipulative and borderline abusive with his high expectations and his lack of respect and love. "I know your parents basically cut her off when she moved to England."

"Yeah. Sarah too, when she dared marry a Brit. At least one without a stock portfolio and connections." He tugged at his earlobe. "That's why I've been building up my own assets outside of him. I've already accumulated some good properties around Boston. And it's why I want to buy something here."

She hadn't even had a chance to run the numbers of his offer. After this wedding. Then she'd know if she even needed to sell. At least for now. "Why? What will all of that lead to?"

"I just don't want to be dependent on him, you know? If he ever decided to disown me too, I'd lose my job, but this way, I wouldn't lose everything. I'm still my own man."

"I don't understand. If he's so awful, why do you keep working for him? Why not escape like your sisters have?" She paused. "Wouldn't it change his father's heart if all of his kids would rather leave than be close?"

Then again, she'd moved back home to be close to hers. And he'd left again.

So.

"Nah. He doesn't care what any of us want. Only what he does." Benjamin blew out a breath. "As for why I stay ... well, I guess I feel like I can better protect my sisters if I'm on the inside, you know? That probably sounds really dumb, but as long as I'm there, the pressure is off of them to be the Bentley heir. Sarah carried that for a long time before she realized she could get away. And he's left her alone for the most part. Let her go. But what happens if I leave too? I'm afraid he'd do something drastic to save face."

"Drastic like what?"

He shrugged. "Blackmail. Trying to meddle in finances. Who knows? He once threatened New Dawn, Sarah's non-profit originally based in Boston, and he's got a pretty long reach."

"No offense, but your sisters seem to be doing a pretty good job of taking care of themselves. Making yourself miserable by staying in a job you hate—working for a man you despise, even if he's your own blood—doesn't seem like something they'd want for you."

"Yeah, well." His mouth swung to the side, his forehead scrunched. "I owe it to them. For a lot of years, I was checked out. And growing up, I never had the same strength my sisters do. Then ..." He sighed. "Well, anyway. I want a relationship with my sisters, so I finally decided to be more than the middle child who went along with everything. More than the guy who hid his pain behind an endless string of meaningless relationships and drinking and playing hard after work every night."

Wow. Maybe there was more to this guy than she'd given him credit for. "I wouldn't say you don't have strength." She nudged him with her shoulder. "After all, you go toe to toe with me, don't you?"

He chuckled. "That's just fun."

"Yes, well, people around here say I'm the Ice Queen, so I figured I was scary or something."

She was teasing but the look he shot down toward her told her he'd figured out the deeper pain she carried. The pain she never let anyone see.

Because once her heart was open, vulnerable, it was that much easier to crush.

"Becs, there's so much more to you than that."

Oh, her heart. "How would you know?" she whispered. "You just met me." Even people who'd known her most of her life would say differently.

"I can just see it."

Blimey. She took a step away, glanced out the window. "Look. The snow has let up." Though it looked like more clouds were coming. "We should go."

Nothing like a warm shower to chase away the chill of snowfall.

Rebecca stepped out of the steamy bathroom and into her bedroom, where she quickly shed her towel and got dressed in stretchy pants and a long-sleeved purple top. Perhaps she should have rented this room out—it was the only bedroom with an attached bath—but she loved being able to hole away completely from the guests if she needed to.

It was only half past five but her stomach grumbled at her. Probably a result of skipping lunch to give Benjamin the tour of Port Willis earlier today. When they'd finally made it back down the hill and through the village covered in white, they'd parted ways, each going to their rooms.

Hopefully she hadn't stolen all the hot water, but she'd stayed in that shower a long time, wishing that these blooming feelings would go away. Recalling every last brutal detail of her breakup with Daniel—a reminder.

Praying that, somehow, the ice around her heart wouldn't melt. That she could remain the Ice Queen, at least until Benjamin left.

Ironic she'd tried doing this in a steaming hot shower, but desperate times, yeah?

Moving back into the bathroom, Rebecca rubbed away the condensation on her mirror. Then she used her towel to press dry her wet hair. It came to her shoulders, was stringy, and—when dry—the dirtiest blonde color she could imagine. Her skin was pale and sometimes freckled. She was short and had a bit of pudge around her middle—another hazard of her job and love of treats.

And yet, she'd never once wished to be anything else. To be beautiful. Because this was who she was, and if a man didn't like it, tough.

But some part of her itched to pull out the makeup she had stashed away somewhere. To maybe blow dry her hair and curl it. To wow Benjamin. Not because he'd made her feel like she had to. But she almost wanted to make an effort—and that wasn't normal for her.

Who was she kidding? Even her best efforts wouldn't make her into the kind of woman Benjamin was used to. She wasn't stylish, gorgeous, or rail thin.

She was just … Rebecca.

And this infatuation that had sprouted out of nowhere inside of her was completely barmy. "Get over it, Rebecca," she said to the mirror.

Disgusted with herself, she tossed the towel aside, made her way through her bedroom, and exited. Time to eat.

When she arrived at the kitchen, she found Benjamin standing just outside the door, his back to her. She cleared her throat and he turned, smiled. "I didn't go into your kitchen uninvited this time."

She couldn't help herself. "So you just decided to hang around outside of it like a creepy bloke?"

"I thought it would be more creepy to knock on your bedroom door. And I have a favor to ask."

"Oh?" Rebecca moved into the kitchen and motioned for him to follow.

"Ginny called. They've got dinner with one of Steven's clients, but their sitter just canceled at the last minute."

"That's awful." Rebecca grabbed some turkey and cheese, some homemade bread, and started to assemble sandwiches. "So what's the favor?"

"I was wondering if you'd mind if the kids came here tonight."

She paused, cheese dangling midair. "Wait. You're going to watch them?"

"Or … *we* could. Together." He held up his hands. "I know you need to keep the place clean, but watching them at Gin's isn't an option since the guests will be having dinner there. The sitter was going to watch them at her house but her own kids are sick. Sarah and Michael are doing something with his family tonight, or she'd have asked them, not the bachelor uncle. But …" He shrugged. "I'm glad I can be here for stuff like this. At least for the week. You know? I've never watched my nieces on my own. I'd like to get to know them better. It's why I'm here."

How could she say no to that? She bit the inside of her cheek as she finished up the sandwiches. "You'd have to help me clean up in the morning before you leave."

"Of course." He cocked his head. "You'll help me, then? To watch them, I mean? I confess, I don't really know that much about kids."

"You were good with them the other night." Rebecca plated the sandwiches and handed one to Benjamin.

"That was different. Their parents were here to be responsible for them." He took a bite of her offering and closed his eyes. "I don't know how you manage to make a simple sandwich taste this good, but I declare you henceforth and forever the Goddess of Food."

"Stop." She shoved him playfully and then slid onto one of the stools with her plate. "I don't really know much about kids either. I've only been around my niece and nephew a handful of times myself. But Ginny's kids are wonderful."

He sat on the stool beside her and chewed thoughtfully. His tangerine cologne floated under her nose, and the hair on her arms stood on end. "Do you want kids of your own someday?"

Choking on a bite, she stood and grabbed a water bottle from the fridge. Unscrewed the cap and took a sip. Then looked back at Benjamin, who studied her. Might as well be honest with the guy. "I'm thirty-seven, so that ship might have sailed by now."

"Don't some women have babies into their forties?"

She handed him his own water bottle and retook her seat. "Maybe, but I know I wouldn't want to single parent." No going the sperm donor route for her, thanks.

"And you don't ever see yourself … I don't know." His thumbnail scratched at the water bottle label. "Getting married?"

Why did that question send a rush of tingles up her spine? Or maybe it was the way he asked it. Like it was more than mere curiosity.

Like her answer meant something to him.

"Getting married would require being in a rela-tionship. And I don't really date." She waggled her eyebrows. "There aren't exactly a lot of eligible men around here."

"There was that Luke guy." Benjamin took

another bite of sandwich but watched her, almost as if gauging her reaction.

"I'm pretty sure he has a thing for Georgiana. And besides, he's at least ten years younger than me."

"What do you have against younger guys?"

"Nothing, but that's *too* much younger for me."

"So if a guy was, say, thirty-five?" he asked. "For example."

He was thirty-five, wasn't he? She narrowed her gaze. "Nope. I find thirty-five-year-olds to be particularly annoying."

He laughed. "Good thing I'm thirty-four."

"Even worse." Rebecca took another swig of water.

"But what if you met a thirty-four-year-old who ended up being your perfect man? The love of your life."

"I don't plan to fall in love with anyone."

"In my experience—which, granted, is quite narrow since I only recently began thinking about actual quality relationships—love isn't usually something you plan."

"No, but it's something you can avoid." She bit into her own sandwich. Her tongue embraced the salty cheese. "I've become quite effective at that in recent years."

"Why is that?"

Oh, no way was she telling him about Daniel. He'd think she was even more pathetic than he likely already did. "What time did you say the kids were coming?"

"So good at changing the subject. But just you wait. I'm gonna wear you down, Rebecca Trengrouse."

She sincerely hoped not.

"Who wants more popcorn?" Rebecca held up a bright red bowl as she walked into the dining room.

"Me!" All three girls and Benjamin cried from their spots at the table. They were all crowded around a kids' puzzle Rebecca had dug up from the games closet. The jungle scene was mostly complete, though Macy looked a bit wiggly and not so much into it.

She perked up when Rebecca set the popcorn in front of her. "Thanks, Auntie Becs."

When Ginny and Steven had adopted Macy over a year ago—followed quickly, to their surprise, by the older twins—they'd started referring to Rebecca in such a way. And even though she pretended like it didn't affect her, every time she heard one of their sweet voices call her that, it broke a little chunk of ice off her heart.

Was she being stubborn by pretending she wasn't part of the family? Maybe selfish too. After everything this child had been through in her short life, didn't she deserve all the love she could get?

Even if it was from someone like Rebecca.

"You're welcome, love." She patted the girl's shoulder and then moved behind Benjamin, who had been the hero of the evening—giving piggyback rides, racing with the girls up and down the stairs, challenging them to marshmallow duels, and being the best uncle three little girls could imagine.

Rebecca spotted a puzzle piece in front of Benjamin and the place it belonged in the picture. Without thinking, she leaned forward over his shoulder to grab it—and stopped when she realized they were cheek to cheek.

"Hi there," he said, teasing.

"Um, I just ..." She straightened, piece in hand, and walked around the table to an open spot between the twins. Her cheeks burned—from embarrassment, from his touch—while she put the piece into place. The girls chattered on, oblivious to Benjamin's gaze on Rebecca.

To the hot string of tension that connected them as she blinked back at him.

She had to get away. "How would you girls like to play hide and seek?" It was the perfect game. She could hide away and never be found—at least until she got her daft heart under control.

Macy pumped her fist, and Lila's and Jessie's faces lit up.

Benjamin sat back in his seat, his eyes not leaving her—as if, once again, he knew what she was thinking. He stroked his chin. "How about a twist on the classic game?"

Her eyebrows shot up. "What twist?"

"Ever heard of sardines?"

The girls hadn't, and neither had Rebecca. So Benjamin explained. "Instead of one person seeking and the rest hiding, only one person hides. When you find that person, you hide with them until only one seeker is left. You guys wanna try it?"

"Yes!" Lila and Jessie jumped up and down.

"It sounds a little scary," Macy admitted.

Rebecca reached across the table for her hand, squeezed. "You can stay with me if you'd like, love."

"Actually"—Benjamin interjected—"I think you should be the hider first since you know all the best hiding spots here."

"Yeah, and Macy, you can stay with me." Lila smiled shyly at her little sister as she stood from the table.

"Okay!" Macy raced over and hugged Lila.

The scene broke a little something inside Rebecca—at the love and care even these siblings had for each other despite knowing each other less than a year. She forced herself to remain stoic lest she completely lose it and scare the children. Clapping her hands, she nodded. "Alright, then. I'll hide. You guys go by the reception desk and close your eyes. Count to fifty. No going outside. No going in the attic. Sound good?"

Benjamin saluted her, a twinkle in his eye. "You got it, Cap."

She rolled her eyes at him, then waited for them to make their way toward the front door and turn. When they started counting, she eased her way up the stairs. Where to hide, where to hide? She could go in her bathroom shower, but she hadn't really cleaned up in there and didn't want Benjamin to see it.

Hmmm. What about the hall closet? No, too obvious.

Oh! There was her kitchen walk-in pantry. But then she'd have to go back downstairs. And it might already be too late for that—

"Ready or not, here we come!"

Blimey. She was out of time. Rebecca scurried down the hallway as quietly as she could and ducked into the first room she came to.

Blinked in the dark and raced for the closet.

Closed it behind her.

And immediately smelled the ocean—and citrus.

"Rebecca, you fool," she hissed into the dark. Because she most definitely was hiding in Benjamin's closet, surrounded by his shirts and coats. It smelled like heaven in here.

Also. It wasn't exactly the most spacious closet, especially with the dresser she'd crammed in here since the room was an odd shape and didn't allow for much furniture in the actual bedroom.

How would multiple people fit in here? She should have picked a larger space. Maybe she still had the chance—

The bedroom door creaked open. Someone was coming. It was too late to move.

Her heart thudded in the dark, the only light a bit of moon-glow streaming through the clouds, through the lone window in the room, through the cracks in the closet door.

Rebecca held her breath.

Then suddenly the closet door opened and a large figure towered over her. "Found you." And before Rebecca could warn him about the squish, he moved inside and shut the door behind him.

And proceeded to smash her against his chest.

To keep herself from falling backward, she wrapped her arms around his waist and crushed her cheek against him. The backs of her legs pressed into his suitcase.

"Not that I mind." His chest rumbled beneath her ear. "But you want to move back a bit there, Beckaroo?"

"I can't. There isn't room."

He chuckled. "Ah, I get it now."

From her awkward angle, she looked up at his face. Couldn't see anything but the outline of his strong nose. "Get what?"

"You planned this so you could have an excuse to cozy up to me. I don't blame you." He let his arms fall around her back, tugging her even closer. Cementing her in place. "I am quite irresistible."

"Ugh, you." She tried to pull away, but he held her firmly in place. "Let me go. The game is over."

"Don't be a spoilsport. The girls are still looking." Benjamin maneuvered them sideways so at least she wasn't about to topple backward over his luggage any longer. "We don't want to ruin the game for them. Or for us," he whispered, his voice a throaty tease.

"We can move somewhere else."

"You know, I'm quite flattered that you chose my room above any other. Curious what you'd find in here?"

"What? No! I got flustered, is all, and went into the first room—"

He clucked his tongue at her. "Sure, sure. I get it."

Her whole body was on fire, and all she wanted to do was melt into him. "You really don't." Because *this* was exactly what she'd been trying to avoid.

He stiffened, perhaps at the way her voice twisted upward, a bit choked. Another way she hadn't meant to show her hand. But he had a way of just … knowing. "What's wrong, Becs?"

Becs. He only seemed to call her that when he *wasn't* teasing. When he actually seemed to … care.

She allowed herself to inhale, to sink into him.

Allowed her palms to flatten along his spine, to push upward a bit so that she was settled into his arms—not in a stiffened pose, but relaxed.

Comfortable.

And maybe … more.

His head dipped, and his nose touched her ear. "I've been meaning to ask, but didn't know how. What was it about that building earlier today that made you cry?"

He remembered that? He'd seen her tears?

She inhaled a shaky breath and tilted her chin upward a bit—now her face lingered not so far from his. Blimey. She couldn't see much, but she could tell that he was close. "That used to be Trengrouse Bakery."

"Ah." His thumbs rubbed circles on her back. "And it makes you sad that it's no longer open?"

"Sad. And angry."

"Why angry?"

"Because I always thought …" She sighed. "It doesn't matter."

"If it upsets you, it matters." His warm breath whooshed against her cheek.

Rebecca waited in silence for a bit, gathering her thoughts. Did she really want to keep up this charade, allow this infatuation, this crush, to become more? To tell him something she hadn't ever revealed to a single soul?

So maybe she did. Even if it was foolish.

Maybe … just for this moment … she could forget about keeping him at arms' length. Clearly that wasn't working—quite literally.

And the story just spilled out. "I dreamed of taking over the family bakery. Dreamed of us doing it together. Me, Mum, and him. Then Mum died six years ago …" She sniffed. "And I decided to move back home, to help Dad with the bakery. Maybe, just maybe, to finally mend the fences that had been broken when I left."

He stood with her there, letting her talk. Exactly what she needed.

"He was always so devoted to the bakery. It came first, you know? And I understood its pull, its magic. But I still wish he'd seen me as worthy of his time and attention. I craved it. And he just …" She shrugged. "He never saw."

Benjamin tugged her closer.

"Then, when I came back, I found out that he was shutting down the bakery. I thought your sister had somehow manipulated him. Because how could he shut down the thing that had always meant more to him than …"

"You?"

"Me."

Benjamin sighed. "Sounds like we both have some daddy issues, huh?"

"Guess so." She laughed through her almost-tears. "And then, to make matters even better, I buy the B&B, settle back into town, trying to make something of our relationship—trying to be a good daughter and care for him. And he up and gets remarried, moves to Falmouth to be near his new wife's family."

"He left you alone."

"I don't think he sees it that way."

"I'm so sorry, Becs." Benjamin pressed a kiss to her temple. So gentle. So unlike the playboy she'd imagined him to be. "I know what it is to feel alone."

"You? Mr. Charisma and Charm?"

"I hide it well." Benjamin's nose nudged Rebecca to look up at him once again. The silence crackled between them.

His lips moved closer to hers. Closer. Closer.

Blimey. It was so warm in here. So comfortable.

And she'd let her heart split wide open.

What was she thinking?

"Becs—"

"This was a bad idea, Benjamin."

"I don't—"

The door swung wide, flooding the room, the closet, with light. Three little faces stared up at them, delighted smiles on their faces. "Found you!"

And not a moment too soon.

CHAPTER 6

*W*as there anything left to do other than decorate the cake, clean Benjamin's room—and wait?

Clicking the pen against her teeth, Rebecca leaned over the reception desk and stared at her to-do list.

Clean up the living room and dining table from last night's puzzles and snacks? Check.

Confirm the rehearsal dinner reservation with Michael's parents at The Village Pub? Check.

Put mints and signature Port Willis ornaments from Mavis's store on all the guest room pillows (save those in Benjamin's still-occupied room)? Check.

Eat an unhealthy number of ginger biscuits for breakfast because she couldn't stop thinking about what might have been an almost kiss in the closet? Check.

Alright, so that last one hadn't been on the actual list, but Rebecca most certainly had accomplished it anyway. Ginger was supposed to be calming to the nerves, though, yeah? And between the wedding party coming in today and her ... interaction ... with Benjamin last night, Rebecca's nerves could use all the help they could get.

Speaking of Benjamin, she had yet to see the man and it was nearly his checkout time. She'd best offer him a swift reminder that his presence here was no longer welcome.

Rebecca set down the pen and headed up the stairs. When she got to his room, she lifted a fist. It hovered near the door for a few long seconds before she pounded. No sense in knocking gently. He needed to get up and out of her inn—her life—as soon as possible.

The door flung open and her jaw dropped at the sight of Benjamin wearing nothing but low-strung flannel pants and a grin.

Rebecca tried to move her gaze quickly from his chest—the man certainly did work out, didn't he?—to his face, but the dancing light in his eyes made it quite obvious she hadn't moved quickly enough.

So she whirled on a heel, facing the opposite wall while Benjamin chuckled behind her. "Can I help you, Ms. Trengrouse?"

"You can get dressed, for starters."

"I wouldn't want to deprive you of this view."

If glares could burn holes in walls like Superman's X-ray vision … "Benjamin Bentley, put a shirt on, for goodness's sake. And then get your things out of this room, because my wedding party arrives in just a few short hours."

He didn't say anything about the hard edge of her voice, but she refused to check whether he was offended or amused. This man had already taken more of her emotional energy than she had to offer. Definitely more than she was willing to give.

Inhaling a deep breath, Rebecca proceeded back through the hallway, down the steps, and toward the kitchen. Cake. She needed to start decorating the cake.

The bell over the front door let loose a merry jingle, grating on Rebecca's last nerve. Surely the wedding party hadn't arrived yet …

But no, it was merely Ginny's redheaded husband and Sophia's husband William—and they were carrying none other than Rebecca's cake layers and frosting.

William's blond curls were peppered with snowflakes. "Gin and Soph asked us to bring these over."

She smacked the side of her head. How could she have forgotten to pick those up? There was nothing for it. The closet scene with Benjamin—which had replayed in her mind on a loop all night long, whether she was awake or asleep—had short-circuited her brain.

"Ah, thanks, mates. You can bring those in here." Rebecca led the way into the kitchen and held open the door.

The men followed, setting the three large layers and the container of buttercream frosting down on the island. Steven dusted off the snow-covered shoulders of his jacket. "Need anything else?"

"No, I'm good." Rebecca cocked her head. "Is it snowing again?" She hadn't set a foot outside since her and Benjamin's trek to the lighthouse yesterday afternoon. Hadn't looked at weather forecasts, either—there hadn't been time or opportunity.

And, to be honest, she didn't want to know what *might* be coming. Assumptions and intentions were all well and good, but she had to deal with what *was*.

"Yeah, it's really coming down out there now," Steven said.

"In all the years I've lived in Cornwall, I'm not sure I've ever seen snow like this." William's eyebrows raised. "The plow from Falmouth was here last night, but it'll have to come back tonight at this rate."

It snowed so infrequently that they shared one plow between three villages. "Seriously?" What did this mean for her event? Rebecca sucked on her bottom lip. She should call Dora and check in.

"Thanks, guys. Appreciate this."

"No problem." Steven clapped William on the shoulder. "Has Sophia converted you to coffee yet? Gin makes a mean cappuccino and I'm craving one."

"She thinks she has but I still prefer my Earl Grey."

Good man. Coffee was of the devil.

The men laughed as they left the kitchen—and then it was just Rebecca and her cake layers.

And the worry building in her gut.

She *should* call Dora—but maybe not until she'd calmed herself with a little cake therapy.

Rebecca tossed on her favorite white apron and gathered what she'd need—a cake leveler for torting, a turntable, cake boards, her offset spatula, her icing smoother, pastry bags, decorating tips—before unwrapping the cake layers.

Then, she began making something from nothing.

Her hands took over and she fell into a rhythm, forgetting everyone and everything but this pink marbled cake with a fondant floral arrangement on top.

A knock sounded on the kitchen door and her gaze darted to the clock over it. How long had she been at this? It was only eleven, so that couldn't be the wedding party. They weren't set to arrive until three.

Benjamin.

"Come in," she called, her hands a bit smudged with the frosting she'd been smoothing out after arranging the cake layers just so.

The man himself stuck his head inside, caught a glimpse of the cake, and whistled. "I am sincerely considering crashing this wedding. That cake looks out of this world."

She stepped back, squinted. It was nothing yet—but it *would* be something. "Have you vacated your room?"

"Wow, okay," He moved into the kitchen. "All business, I see."

"What else would I be?" She turned back to the cake and studied it again. Found a spot that needed smoothing. Picked up her spatula and took care of it.

There.

Now all she needed to do was add the pizzazz. The wow factor.

Even though Benjamin had already given it his approval—his wow—in its unfinished state. He saw its potential.

Saw her potential too.

"Becs, there's so much more to you than that."

She shuddered at the memory of his words, the way he'd touched her soul in just his short time here.

It was good he was leaving. Right. He belonged in America.

"Alright, well." Benjamin stepped closer.

She willed herself to stay frozen, staring at the cake. "Well."

"My suitcase is all packed up, so the room is yours again. I guess I just need my final bill and you can get me all checked out."

She nodded, set down her spatula, and wiped her hands on her apron before pushing a loose strand of hair from her eyes. "Follow me." Easing past him, she fled the kitchen and headed for the reception desk.

Where her phone vibrated.

Rebecca picked it up. Oh no.

Five missed calls—from Dora.

And a voicemail.

Her fingers shaking, Rebecca pushed the button to listen and brought the phone to her ear. "Rebecca. Hi." Dora's voice sounded tearful, tinny—or maybe that was just the shock factor of her mind trying to shield Rebecca from what she knew was coming. "I'm so sorry to do this, but … the storm is just too bad. We have to cancel our wedding. Well—" Dora hiccupped. "We aren't canceling it. We're just moving it here. I can't stand to wait another day to marry Travis, but there's absolutely no way to make it safely to Port Willis. And—oh, you're simply going to hate me—Trav told me I need to invoke the clause you allowed in the contract for cancelation due to weather."

Rebecca's heart thrummed. "No."

"What is it?" Benjamin's hand was on her arm in an instant, his eyebrows sky-high.

Rebecca just shook her head.

"Of course, we'll pay for the food you've surely already purchased, and any expenses you've incurred securing items or decor for the wedding, but anything else …"

Insides numb, Rebecca listened to the rest of the message—a bunch of platitudes and apologies that wouldn't help.

That wouldn't redeem the fact that she'd just lost her only chance at paying off a huge chunk of her loan in one fell swoop.

In enough time.

She lowered the phone and turned to her computer, hands erratic as they clicked around, pulled up the Donaldson contract, scrolled to the clause Dora had mentioned.

Why, oh why, hadn't she asked an attorney—Sarah would have helped, if only she'd buried her stupid pride—to look over the contract? The groom had suggested a few amendments to the contract template the B&B's previous owner had left for Rebecca, and she hadn't thought anything of them.

Had been so desperate for a client, an event—her big break—that she'd ignored the risk.

"Becs, what's wrong?" Benjamin asked again, this time a bit more forcefully.

Why did the man care? He was leaving in less

than a week. Sure, he'd offered to buy this place, but whether he did or didn't, it wouldn't change the trajectory of *his* career. He'd continue to be a wealthy, important man from Boston.

But this … this was Rebecca's *life*.

And everything had just gone up in smoke.

"My wedding party … they canceled." Tears threatened to pool in her eyes, to fall. She blinked fiercely against them.

"Aw, man. I'm so sorry."

The fact he didn't tease her about him being able to stay said something. She just wasn't sure what. Maybe he knew that she couldn't take any jokes right now.

Benjamin squeezed her arm. "At least it isn't a total loss, though. Canceling this last minute has to have consequences, right? What's the cancelation fee?"

"Nothing."

"Come again?"

She pursed her lips. "I let them write this clause into the contract—the groom's a lawyer, and I was so …" Looking at the ceiling, she inhaled against the almost-there tears. "Anyway, basically, if the weather prevents them from getting here, they get a full refund."

"But that's absurd. Surely you didn't agree to that." Ben's voice trailed off as he caught the scathing look she shot him. "Let me see the contract."

"Be my guest." She pointed to the computer, then hurried back to the kitchen. Whatever he was doing wouldn't change a thing.

Hitting the door with the hilt of her hand—ow— she returned to the cake. The beautiful, half-completed cake. The one that was going to be a masterpiece.

Now, it never would reach its potential.

Rebecca held back a scream. She felt like smashing something.

Her eyes narrowed in on the cake. Breath coming quickly, she picked up a spatula and held it in her fist as she advanced on the blasted thing.

"Don't you dare ruin that wonderful creation with your pent-up rage."

She turned, glared at Benjamin. "Why not? All of this work—down the pan. What does it matter now?"

Benjamin stalked into the kitchen and snatched the spatula from her before she could react. He held it above her head.

"Give that back." She jumped for it, but he continued to hold it out of reach. Dodgy scoundrel. Using his height advantage to be cruel. "If I want to destroy this cake, I'll do it."

"I've got a much better idea." Benjamin set the spatula on top of the fridge—well out of Rebecca's reach—and pulled open a nearby drawer, pulling out a pair of forks.

Her hands found her hips. "Are you actually suggesting—"

"—that we eat this masterpiece as God intended rather than decimate it some other way?" He moved until he was just next to her, then handed her a fork. Winked. "Yes. I absolutely am."

She'd never eaten so much cake in one sitting in her life.

Rebecca groaned and leaned back against the couch. "I can't believe you made me do that." With her foot, she pushed the white plate of cake crumbs farther away on the coffee table.

Benjamin forked another piece of his own cake and popped it into his mouth before setting his plate on the side table next to him. After swallowing, he shook his finger at her. "I may have forced that first piece on you, but the second? The third?" He grinned. "That was all you, Beckaroo."

She took the decorative pillow beside her and covered her face with it, temporarily blocking out the roaring fireplace, the Christmas tree covered in ornaments and lights, the window out which snow fell in droves. "Don't remind me. My stomach hates me."

"But the rest of you feels just a bit better, doesn't

it?" Benjamin pulled at the pillow, bringing it back down to her lap.

And now, instead of the cozy living room, she was staring at his crinkled brown eyes, his white teeth, his Grecian nose.

His highly symmetrical lips.

She ripped her gaze away from him, hugging the pillow to her middle. "I guess." Benjamin had been sweet, helping her to get her mind off of the Donaldson cancelation. They'd spent most of the last hour inhaling the cake and talking about completely random things like their favorite Christmas movies, songs, and drinks.

Not surprisingly, they didn't agree, which made it all the more fun.

She wasn't sure when it had happened, but arguing with Benjamin was quickly becoming Rebecca's new favorite thing.

But even light-hearted banter wasn't enough to ward off the chilly thoughts about her future here at the B&B.

The logs in the fireplace shifted and the flames crackled. "I really needed that money." Rebecca sniffled. Ugh. "And you're right. I was absurd to let them add that clause. But it never snows here. Not like this. And I … I needed it so badly."

"First, I'm sorry I said that it was absurd." Benjamin twisted sideways, and the cushion underneath him dipped and squeaked as he pulled one leg up onto the couch beneath him. "And second, why do you need it so much?"

If she was truthful, she risked him rescinding his offer to buy the inn. And though she hadn't had much time to consider the offer in detail, it might be her only option next to bankruptcy.

Still, after how nice he'd just been to her, he deserved her honesty.

"I got in over my head." Lowering the pillow to her lap once more, she told him about the loan. About all the cancelations this last year. About the economic decline. About her aversion toward marketing. "I know you might find this hard to believe, but I generally don't like people."

"I had no idea." His foot nudged hers as he flashed her a grin. "I thought it was just me."

"You're the worst." She forced a smile. "But yes, I suppose I've earned my moniker as the Ice Queen of Port Willis."

"Okay, I can see how some might find you a bit standoffish, but you're not *that* bad."

"A glowing endorsement. Rebecca Trengrouse—not that bad." At that, she finally laughed.

"Atta girl. See? Would an ice queen laugh at herself?" Benjamin leaned his head against his arm, which rested along the back of the couch. "So why don't you like people?"

She chewed the inside of her lip. "I guess it's not

so much about liking people as depending on them. Letting them in."

"And why don't you want to do that?"

Something in his voice made her want to turn to him, to lean in close, to let him hold her. But she couldn't do that.

Because it would lead absolutely nowhere.

Still, despite his playboy reputation, Benjamin had never been anything but sweet to her. He didn't flash his wealth like she'd expect him to. He didn't take himself too seriously. And he asked about her, as if he really cared.

If he was simply looking for someone to mess around with, he could have gone after sweet Charlotte or sexy Georgiana.

But he was here, with Rebecca.

She wasn't the woman for him—she couldn't be—but on the off chance he really did care for her, she wanted him to know why she couldn't open her heart to him.

Rebecca turned her head, pressing her cheek against the back couch cushion. "People leave, Benjamin."

"Not always."

"Alright, well, they always leave me. Dad. Blake. Mum, in her own way. And before all of them, Nana."

"Was that your grandma?"

She nodded. "Nana was the one person who

understood me. Who took the time to really know who I was, what I wanted. *She* knew I wanted to take over the bakery someday, and she helped train me for it. When my parents were too busy running the bakery, Nana took me under her wing and taught me how to bake everything—pies, biscuits, cakes. Until …"

He covered her hand on top of the pillow. Squeezed. "Until?"

"Until she got sick when I was eleven. Then she …" Rebecca's voice shook and she swallowed. The phantom taste of leftover cake haunted her mouth, the frosting now sickly sweet. "One day, maybe a week after her funeral, Dad found me crying. I know he was trying to comfort me, to say something helpful—or maybe he was just tired of my tears—but he said, 'This is the cost of loving people. A broken heart when they're gone.'"

Letting go of her fingers, Benjamin arched toward the side table and picked up a tissue, which he brought back to her hand.

"Thanks." The tissue came away mascara black when she swiped under her eyes. "You know, most kids would hear that and think, true. Loving people *does* cost something, but it's something I'm willing to pay."

"But not you?"

Rebecca shook her head. "Instead, my first instinct was to protect myself. To say, 'If love hurts,

I'm not going to do it.' I didn't ever want to face that prison of pain again. Because I knew I wasn't strong enough to endure another broken heart." She averted her eyes again. Gusts of snow batted at the window next to the Christmas tree. It was only early afternoon, and yet the clouds obscured most of the sunlight. "And I was right."

Because a woman didn't agree to marry a man without losing a bit of her heart to him. Somehow, Daniel had gotten past Rebecca's radar.

And proved her right in the end.

"What do you mean?"

She shouldn't be telling him this. But the confessions had been pushing, bucking, ready to spill out of her, and she was tired of fighting them. The floodgates opened and out the story came. "Let's just say I was engaged once and it didn't work out."

"Wow, I'm sorry. What happened?"

She sighed. "He broke up with me the day before our wedding. Ten years together and he never once expressed doubts. But that day ..." She turned back to Benjamin. "That day he told me for the first time that he didn't think he could marry someone like me."

Benjamin's jaw clenched. "Sounds like you dodged a bullet."

"Or he did."

"No. Definitely you." He studied her. Practically

snarled. *"Someone like you* … that guy didn't know what he had. You're one of a kind, Becs."

Her jaw dropped. How did this guy not hate her for the way she'd treated him since the moment he'd arrived? Why had he bothered to look deeper? Maybe it was a Bentley trait, because Ginny hadn't written her off either.

They'd seen she was covering up something.

"Ben…"

His eyes sharpened as she breathed out the casual version of his name. "Yeah?"

"Just … thank you. For saying that."

"I only speak the truth."

They stared at each other for several long, quiet moments. Nothing—and yet everything—between them.

Finally, Benjamin cleared his throat. "To go back to what you said earlier about love not being worth the hurt—I understand what you mean. But the thing is, not loving is a prison of its own kind."

Her mouth opened to ask him what he meant, but she instantly shut it instead. He'd been so patient to simply let her process. To let her speak when she was ready.

This time, she reached for his hand.

His eyes widened slightly.

But he threaded their fingers together and held on for several long moments before speaking again.

"I told you how my dad is a hard man. A selfish, greedy man."

She nodded.

"I still remember the moment as a kid when I decided to be nothing like him. I was in junior high, and I'd worked really hard on a speech for the student council election. On the campaign as a whole, really. Well, I got up there, gave my speech, and shook hands like I was running for the President of the United States."

Rebecca grinned at the thought of a young Benjamin using his swagger in an awkward teen body—if he'd ever had one of those. Given how he'd turned out as an adult, she had her doubts.

"Anyway, one of our teachers came up to me afterward and congratulated me on how well I'd done. 'You're definitely George Bentley's son—the spitting image!'"

"Ouch."

His eyebrows folded together. "Yeah. After that, I did everything possible to not be him. Until college, when he practically forced me to pursue an MBA. Even then, I'm fairly certain he paid off my professors for good grades, because I definitely didn't study much."

"Good thing you're so naturally intelligent, then." Rebecca knocked a fist lightly against his head, laughing.

"I'm glad you recognize it." His grin flashed, then

faded. "Unfortunately, I wasn't always the smartest with the choices I made for my life. Even though I actually did go to work for my dad, I didn't want to be seen as a hard-nosed executive like he is."

"That sounds smart, actually."

"So surprised." He tapped her nose. "On the one hand, I think I'm a good boss. I don't rule by fear like he does. But on the other hand, I partied with my employees. A lot. And the women I've dated, they didn't have substance. Not like …" Benjamin's eyes bore into her.

Aaaaand there came the stomach swoops again.

Blimey. "So what changed? You make it sound as if that's all in the past."

"It is." Benjamin squeezed her fingers. "I got a wake-up call. See, one day I realized that despite all my efforts to avoid being the man George Bentley is, I was exactly like him. Maybe not abusive or manipulative, but selfish—which, really, is the root of his problems. I'd held myself back from really caring about anyone except me. About my own desires. And that made me literally sick. I threw up for a few days after figuring that one out."

What kind of man actually admitted things like this? She shouldn't ask more—didn't want to push— but she had to know. Mining the depths of who Benjamin Bentley was … it was becoming addictive.

Maybe she'd strike gold.

Or maybe she'd end up empty-handed.

But right now, she didn't care about that. She only cared about him. "What happened to make you realize all of that?"

Benjamin shifted slightly, facing forward. He still held her hand, but it felt like he was pulling away. "I, um … a girl I'd been with thought she might be pregnant. She wasn't," he rushed on. "But she wanted to get married. And I could tell she had real feelings for me. Meanwhile, I'd been the jerk who was just messing around." He swallowed hard. "The thought that I could have brought an innocent kid into a relationship like that, or that maybe we would have made a different decision to avoid the responsibility … it still haunts me, Becs."

Oh, Benjamin. "We've all made mistakes."

"I'm just so grateful God got ahold of my heart after that."

Wait. Benjamin was a man of faith?

She shouldn't be surprised. He wasn't perfect, but he was good. And steady. Just like both of his sisters. "What did He show you?"

"That the way my dad treated me had caused my trust in others to wane, so I'd basically blocked off my heart. But we were designed to need other people. Not just need them, but pour out all the love we have in our hearts." His thumb moved along the delicate edge of her hand. "And I'm not even just talking about romantic relationships. I'm also talking friendships. Relationships with our families

—as long as they're safe and healthy and within our boundaries." His Adam's apple bobbed. Was he thinking of his father? "And our relationship with God. I think … I think that maybe He wants us to trust Him most of all."

She'd made strides toward allowing others in—sitting here with Benjamin was proof of that. But God? That was a mite harder for her. "To be honest, Benjamin, I'm not sure He really cares that much about me."

"How could He not?" Benjamin's eyes shone despite the shrouded light from outside. "He made you. You're His child. He sees you, Becs."

Biting her lip, she pulled her hand away. "Nobody sees me." If they had, they wouldn't have left.

Right?

"You're wrong." The burning look in his eyes confirmed his declaration.

Whoa.

"I don't know how to trust anymore, Benjamin. How to believe." She sighed. "I think I'm broken."

"We're all a little broken, Becs." He smiled. Gentle. Calm. Lovely. "The point is to be broken together. And to help put each other back together, one piece at a time."

CHAPTER 7

Maybe Benjamin was right.

Rebecca stared at her bedroom ceiling, listening to the wind howl outside. All night long she'd lain here doing the same thing, her mind whirling as intensely as the snow outside.

"I think we were designed to need other people. Not just need them, but pour out all the love we have in our hearts."

She'd blamed so many of her problems on her father's lack of love for her—on how easy it was for him to leave her. But had she really ever poured out her love on *him*? After Nana died, a part of Rebecca had too. And she'd allowed it to happen. Except for her attempt with Daniel, she'd never really come back from Nana's death, but had let her relationships shrivel up until the other person couldn't sustain it alone.

She really *was* the Ice Queen.

A tear leaked down her cheek. How had she become this person?

Daniel's final accusation came back to her, smacking her between the eyes—*"I just don't feel you love me as much as I love you. You're cold, Rebecca, and I thought I'd be enough to warm you back up again. But nothing I've done has changed you."*

The part that hurt the most? He was right—all this time. Not that he'd handled things well. That had still left a scar.

But Rebecca needed to own her part in the failed engagement as well.

Blimey. How had a handful of conversations with some random American man over the course of a few days led to more of a breakthrough than a ten-year relationship?

For the first time in a long time, Rebecca wondered what it might be like to try—really try—to step back into a life with others. Ginny had been the only one she'd really let close, but even there she'd put up walls.

But what if … what if she did what Benjamin said? What if she let people in? What if she let Blake in?

Even … Dad.

Was that possible?

Her heart skipped at the thought and Rebecca

wrenched her quilt back, sitting up and putting on her slippers.

She was going to do it. She was going to go visit Dad today—before she lost her nerve. He'd called enough times. Maybe she could bring him a pie, check on him.

Surely the storm would have passed by now. They never lasted long in Port Willis.

Rebecca bolted from her room and ran down the stairs, which creaked with each drop of her weight onto the wood. She shivered as she entered the living room area—when had it gotten so cold down here?

Snatching her phone off the charger, Rebecca peeked at her call log. Yep, there. A missed call from Dad. Yesterday.

She unlocked the phone and walked to the front door to check whether the Falmouth snowplow had come through yet. Maybe she could even make it over to Falmouth for a late breakfast. Lunch, at the very least.

As Rebecca opened the door, her hand dropped— as did her jaw.

This couldn't be happening.

Snow. Everywhere. Piled high on the pavements, the street. Covering the few vehicles she saw, only the top halves visible.

And it was still coming down. The sky tossed it

down like confetti—but there was nothing to celebrate.

What twilight zone had she entered?

No one ever got snowed in in Port Willis. Blizzards didn't happen here. They just … didn't.

The possible had become so much more than probable.

It had actually happened.

"Are you going to keep standing there staring at the snow and letting all the warm air out?"

She turned. Benjamin sat tucked into one of the reading chairs beside the fire, which was newly lit after their time together last night. After yesterday's cozy confessions on the couch, Benjamin and Rebecca had watched *A Christmas Story*—just to stay occupied. With the snow blowing like it had been outside, there wasn't much else they *could* do.

Since she didn't have a television downstairs, Benjamin had pulled out his laptop and set it on the coffee table in front of them. She'd purposefully put her feet up on the couch and turned so her back was against the sofa's arm.

Then she'd tucked a blanket all around herself so he couldn't even feign an innocent touch. Because despite their moments together yesterday, the man still had a return plane ticket on December twenty-sixth. And Rebecca felt herself falling for him.

Harder and harder, minute by minute.

The landing was going to hurt whenever her heart decided to come back to earth.

She cleared her throat and closed the door. "I think we're snowed in."

A grin curved his lips. "Chin up, Beckaroo. I'm not that bad."

No. He wasn't.

And that was the problem—a problem made even more precarious by the fact she wouldn't be able to escape him today.

Maybe not even tomorrow. Who knew how long this weather was going to keep up.

At least they still had electricity.

"Just because we shared some cake doesn't mean I want to be stuck with you any longer than I have to be." She said it as straight-faced as she could, but his eyes lit up—he knew she was lying. Teasing.

And her dumb heart leaped at the sight.

Rebecca headed for the kitchen. She had muffins and biscuits galore thanks to her prep for the wedding, but a hot slice of banana loaf smothered in butter sounded infinitely better. Besides, it would give her a way to rid her body of this extra tension.

She got out the ingredients, but before she even had a chance to plug in her mixer to cream the butter and sugar, Benjamin entered after her. Rebecca tsked at him. "You know guests are supposed to—"

"Wait outside the kitchen. I know." He headed

into her walk-in pantry and emerged with one of her black aprons.

"What, may I ask, are you doing with that?"

"What does it look like?" He slipped it over his head, and the top loop caught on his hair, mussing the back. She had the strong urge to push it down. The apron was impossibly small on him, hugging his middle like a kid clinging to his mother's leg. "I'm helping."

She snorted. "No."

"Aw, come on. Give me a chance." He rubbed his hands together as he approached the stand mixer and peeked inside. "What are we making?"

She pushed him out of the way and plugged it into the outlet on the island. "*We* are not making anything. *I* am making a banana loaf."

"Please, Becs?" He tried to step back into the spot where she stood, and his scent—plus the leftover splashes of sugar and vanilla on the apron—invaded all of her senses.

She cocked her head, tapped her chin as if actually considering letting him handle her kitchen equipment—which was laughable. "What kind of baking experience do you have?"

"Absolutely none. But I'm a very good student."

This man was going to be the death of her. "Fine. But do everything exactly as I say."

"Right-O, Cap'n."

"And lose the outrageously awful accent."

He placed a hand on his broad chest. "It's not awful. I sound just like you."

She rolled her eyes and smiled. How did he do that? Just minutes ago, she'd been despairing over the snow. But Benjamin—plus the prospect of baking—made her forget.

"Here." After peeling two bananas, she placed them into a bowl and shoved a fork at him. "Mash those while I cream the sugar and butter."

"Cream them? Like beat them up real good?" Despite his goofy question, he did as she asked.

"Yes, just like that." She measured and dumped the sugar into the mixing bowl, then added softened butter before turning the mixer on. Her shoulders relaxed as the appliance purred and filled the kitchen with white noise.

Benjamin came up behind her, peeked down over her shoulders. His fingers brushed her lower back, and she bit her cheek at the fire that spread from that spot up and out to every cell in her body. "Look. It's getting all light and fluffy."

The awe in his voice, like a young boy at the North Pole, made her turn slightly, look back and up at him. "A bit more delicate than beating it up, hmm?" She turned the mixer off and picked up the two eggs. "Want to crack these in?"

"I don't want to get eggshells in the bowl."

"You'll be fine."

Still standing behind her, he reached for one of

the eggs. His hand skimmed hers, kept touch a moment longer than necessary. "You know those movies when a man is teaching a woman how to swing a golf club, and he takes hold of her hands to guide her?"

"Yes …" Where was he going with this?

Then he placed his other arm around her other side, so she was trapped in his embrace, though both of them faced forward. "You might need to pretend these eggs are a golf club."

He was teasing her, she knew, but there was some part of her that wanted to play along.

Instead, she ducked under his left arm and patted him on the back. "You've got this. I believe in you."

Benjamin sighed as if he was the most long-suffering man alive, then attempted to crack the eggs one-handed into the bowl.

Instead, he completely crushed them in his fists. The yolks eked out between his closed fingers and glopped into the bowl, tiny bits of shells and all. "Oops."

And Rebecca couldn't help it—she guffawed. Bent in two as she clutched her stomach. Tears came —the laughing-so-hard kind—and dripped down her nose onto the tile below.

"Oh sure. Laugh at the guy who was raised with no practical skills but started economics and accounting at age seven."

Even though she heard the joking in his voice,

she stopped laughing, straightened, and swiped at her tears. Then she walked over to snag some paper towels and handed them to Benjamin. "Your mum really never showed you how to cook anything?"

He shot her a wry grin as he took the towels and began cleaning off his hands. "You presume that Mariah Bentley knows how."

"Wow." That was so foreign to her life growing up. "I think I was cracking eggs at age three."

"It sounds like a lot of your happiest memories revolve around baking with your loved ones."

"Yeah, I guess they do." She peeked inside the mixing bowl. Was anything salvageable? Nope. Tiny shells had seeped into the mixture. They needed to start over. But they had all day, didn't they? "And you know, I didn't think I'd get many more of them. But what you said last night really got me thinking." She detached the bowl from the mixer and took it over to the rubbish bin, where she scooped the gloopy mess inside.

Now at the sink, Benjamin finished washing his hands clean. Dried them. Then made his way back to her, still quiet. Not even teasing her for how brilliant he was for giving her something to think about.

Still just giving her the space to process.

She quickly washed out the bowl, dried it, and carried it back to the mixer stand. They could make the bread another time. This was important.

Hopping up on the counter, she faced Benjamin.

"I think I've been stuck. And … I'm ready to move forward. To maybe make more memories."

"Yeah?" He took a step forward until he was just in front of her. Then he lifted a hand and tucked a piece of her hair behind her ear. "What kind of memories?"

Blimey. Did he think she meant … with him?

Though they *had* just made some wonderful memories—a baking session she'd surely not forget anytime soon. If at all.

"Um." She chewed on her bottom lip and Benjamin's pupils darkened as his gaze wandered to her mouth.

He braced his hands on the counter, one on either side of her, and angled forward. So close the tips of their noses touched. Almost like he wanted to …

"Well." Rebecca licked her lips. When had it become so warm in here? So dry. "I was thinking about calling my dad. Seeing what he's doing for Christmas. Maybe even my brother."

Benjamin blinked. Had she caught him off guard talking about someone other than him and Rebecca?

Not that there *was* a him and Rebecca.

"Oh." He took a step back, ran a hand through his hair. "That's great, Becs. I think it's a great idea. It's just … great." He chuckled, but she didn't miss the flash of hurt in his eyes. Confusion.

Yeah. Great, indeed. She was driving him away.

And she found, in that moment, that she didn't want to. Even if it made no sense, she wanted him close.

Needed him close.

"Wait. Ben." She reached for his shirt and gave a slight tug—enough to show him what she wanted.

And he came willingly, pressing closer, his arms circling her waist, hers finding their way around his neck. They were from different worlds, but right here, right now, somehow they fit—two puzzle pieces that had been separated. Now joined.

Benjamin's face moved closer again, his nose nudging hers until her eyes slipped closed. And then his lips found the corner of her mouth, and he kissed her there. Soft. Feather like.

But still enough to bowl her over.

Then he moved his focus to the other corner of her mouth. She shuddered at the connection, light as it was.

And finally, his mouth met hers inch for inch for the briefest of moments before he pulled away, looked fully into her eyes. "Was that … is that okay?"

She was just about to answer a resounding—and likely overenthusiastic—"Yes!" when the lights flickered above them.

Flickered … and died.

This was a terrible idea. But it was also practical. And Rebecca Trengrouse was nothing if not practical.

Had she ever wanted Benjamin to set foot in her room? No. It was her safe place. And it made her feel vulnerable for someone else to see her unmade bed, the scattering of papers on the desk in the corner, the way she'd left the toothpaste lid off the tube in the bathroom.

And yet, here he was—about to spend the night on the floor in front of her fireplace.

"Are you sure about this?" Hands in his pockets, Benjamin stood in the doorway as Rebecca laid a pile of blankets and quilts on the white rug that covered the wood flooring beneath.

"Of course I'm sure. My bedroom is the only one with a fireplace. How else are you going to keep warm all night?"

"I could sleep downstairs in the living room."

"The ceilings are too high and heat rises." Rebecca grabbed her extra pillow and tossed it on the ground. "Besides, it doesn't make sense to heat multiple rooms in the house."

"I could see if Ginny has room for me."

Sarah's was too far to walk in this blizzard, but Ginny's was just next door. And even though the power lines—and cell towers—weren't working, they'd been able to sneak out to grab firewood from the back of the bakery and visit with Ginny and Steven most of the day.

Anything to avoid being alone with Benjamin after that kiss—the one that, as brief as it was, had turned Rebecca's mind to mush.

But there was no avoiding this. "You know how tiny her living room is, and I have it on good authority that the girls want to do a sleepover in there tonight."

"Excuses, excuses." He clucked his tongue. "I think you just like the idea of sharing a room with me. You sure you can handle this?"

Rebecca rolled her eyes. "Please." They were adults. Was she attracted to him? Sure. Did she like him? Okay, fine, yes.

Had his three-second kiss left her imagining what he could do with three minutes? Three hours? Three days?

Ugh. Unfortunately, yes again.

But somewhere in the last twelve hours, her better judgment had caught up with her. Benjamin Bentley was leaving in four days—and she was going to try to make a life here in Port Willis. One that actually included her family. And friends.

Maybe she'd even attempt to make more of those.

Snagging his arm, she dragged him into the room. "You're letting all the warm air escape." Then she shut the door behind him and turned to grab a pair of wool blankets. "I need your help getting this room insulated for the night. Or did you forget that we are in an emergency situation with no source of heat other than this fire?"

His silly grin disappeared and he took the blankets from her. "Yeah, of course."

She dragged a chair over from her desk in the corner and, grabbing a hammer and some nails she'd drudged up from the recesses of her supply closet, stepped up. Without a word, he handed her the corner of a blanket and she started securing it above the doorway.

They worked in silence to cover the two windows as well, blocking out their view of swirling snow. Now the fireplace served as the only source of light as well as heat. The flames blazed and crackled, the popping cadence filling the silence between them.

It was far too cozy a scene.

But they had no choice.

"Well." Rebecca tossed her thick robe over her flannel pants and crawled into bed, pulling three thick quilts over her. "Good night."

Benjamin stood near her, staring down, and let loose a staccato laugh. Shook his head. "It's not that late, Becs. Why not come sit by the fire and talk?"

Talk? Next to him? That sounded … wonderful.

Too wonderful. She'd likely lose her head again. And then where would she be?

"I'm good here, thanks."

"Suit yourself." Benjamin plopped down in front of her bed, out of Rebecca's view. There was shuffling as he got comfortable on the floor—if such a thing was really possible. She'd briefly considered offering him the other half of her bed, but decided that was a terrible idea. He could suffer the hard ground for one night.

For a long while, they both lay in the quiet. But she couldn't sleep, not just because it was only eight in the evening—if her battery-powered clock was accurate—but because the more time that passed, the more she felt him there. "You awake down there?" she whispered.

"Of course I'm awake, Becs." His voice didn't hold a tease like it normally did.

"I'm sorry it's probably not very comfortable ..."

"That's not it."

Oh? "Then what is it?"

"You really want to know? Or are you going to run away?"

"Where am I going to run?" She tried desperately for a pestering tone—to get them back to the status quo.

But apparently Benjamin was determined to destroy that. Or maybe it was the kiss that had done so. "You can't blame a guy for wondering. You haven't exactly been open to talking today."

She harrumphed in protest.

"What? It's true. After this morning in the

kitchen, I thought … But then you hardly looked at me the rest of the day, kept chatting with my sister and avoiding me—"

"I did not!"

She totally had.

Holding in a groan, she briefly buried her face in her pillow.

"Becs." He said her name so gently. It made her want to cry. To throw aside these quilts and seek comfort in his arms. With him.

But his arms would only be there for so long.

"You're leaving." There. What could he say to that?

He huffed in response. "I don't want to."

"But that doesn't change the fact that you are."

"I'll be back."

"For visits, maybe. When you can get around to seeing your sisters again. Will it be another ten years?" That was a low remark and she knew it the moment the thought left her lips. He wasn't the same man he'd been—his family was important to him.

"Geez, Beckaroo."

"I'm sorry. I know you've changed, but England is a long way from Boston, and you lead a busy life." A busy life very different from the one that belonged to Rebecca.

For several long moments, Benjamin didn't speak. Rebecca shivered despite the bed coverings over her.

Finally, "I know it's far, Becs. And I regret my distance, the way I didn't take time to visit Ginny all of those years …" He sighed, and she could picture him scrubbing a hand down his face. "I also know it's really easy to fall back into old habits, to let myself get so busy with work that I don't take time for what's important. It's why I want to invest in a business here in town. So I'm forced to stay close. So that, even if I struggle to keep my priorities straight, I'll have a tangible something linking me to this town. This place. My family."

Rebecca curled into herself. Her hands fisted the pillow under her head. "That's admirable, Benjamin. But I don't understand how owning a piece of land or a business will keep you coming back. Wouldn't you just hire a manager and turn over the keep of the place to him or her?"

"I …" A pause. "I don't know. I guess I just pictured being more involved than that."

Her heart skipped. "You … you aren't talking about moving here, are you?"

"No."

Oh.

"Not that I wouldn't maybe want to."

OH.

"So …" She cleared her throat. "Why *haven't* you considered that?"

"I already told you, Becs. I can't leave my job. My dad …"

Right. "You want to protect your sisters from him." The fire created dancing shadows of light and dark on the wall, each one competing for dominance. "But I still argue that that's not your responsibility. Your dad makes his own decisions and choices. And you're isolating yourself in order to save everyone else, but didn't you just tell me that we need other people?"

Had she said too much? After all, she was out of practice when it came to speaking into other people's lives.

"I just want to be there for the people I love." His voice was a whisper, so soft she almost didn't hear it.

And yet, the sincerity boomed in her heart, as loud as if he'd shouted the words from the lighthouse.

Here was a good man. Was he struggling under the weight of something that wasn't his to bear? Yes. But he was trying.

And she … she was in a position to help him do the thing he thought he had to do. It would help her too, because now that the Donaldson wedding money wasn't coming in, Rebecca was going to lose the inn without a miracle.

Unless she accepted Benjamin's offer to buy it.

And yes, it meant letting go of the majority of her inheritance. But maybe that wasn't the only thing she'd ever get from her father like she thought. Maybe there was still love to be given and received, if she could just take the steps back toward her family.

Maybe that was her real inheritance. Her real legacy.

"Okay." The word rang with finality. The decision had been made.

"Okay … what?"

Oh, right. Benjamin wasn't privy to the inner workings of her mind—and thank goodness, or he'd know just how much restraint she was using in not abandoning her bed for a snuggle sesh right about now. "Okay, I'll sell the inn to you."

"Wait." Benjamin's head popped over the edge of the bed as he sat up. "Seriously?"

"Yes."

"Are you sure?"

"Why do you keep acting like I don't know my own mind?" First sharing a room for the night, now this. "I'm a grown woman and I said I'll sell the inn to you. Now, if you don't want my magnanimous gift—"

"Gift?" The teasing glint in his voice had returned. "Aren't I the one paying you?"

"—then I'll just sell to some other American dolt who sees what my inn is worth."

"No need for that. I know exactly what it's worth —it *and* its owner." He lay back down. Meanwhile, his words, their meaning, blazed in Rebecca's heart, lighting a path through the darkness. "And I accept."

"Good. Now stop bothering me and go to sleep." She smiled to herself, even as a pang of something fierce and unwanted welled up in her chest.

Benjamin was leaving soon.

And so was she. The question was … where would she go now?

CHAPTER 8

*O*vernight, the world had changed.

And all because the sun had come to stay.

Rebecca turned her face skyward, allowing the warm rays to kiss her cheeks. Despite the definite nip in the air, despite the centimeters upon centimeters of white fluff covering the ground, the sun had changed everything.

As had the agreement she'd made with Benjamin forty hours ago.

"So you're really going to sell to my brother?" Ginny adjusted the kettle sitting over the fire pit grate in her backyard.

Beyond where they sat, huddled in hoodies and blankets, a good old-fashioned snowball fight raged. Steven, Benjamin, and the girls raced around in their snow jackets and pants flinging spheres of white at one another, laughing and marveling at the winter wonderland they'd been given on Christmas Eve.

"I really am. We spent a decent chunk of yesterday hashing out the details as best we could without Internet." The power had returned late last night, though the service from the nearest cell tower had only come back on this morning. By the time they had Internet again, Rebecca's head had ached with all the swirling information that she'd both divulged and taken in.

But it had been better than talking about that kiss.

Thankfully, Benjamin hadn't brought it up again. Not like they'd exactly discussed in length what it had meant—or anything other than the fact she'd avoided him immediately after it had happened.

Still, it was better this way.

Acknowledging it made the kiss—and the feelings that went along with it—real.

"So what are you going to do now?" The kettle whistled and Ginny lifted it off the fire pit before pouring it into disposable cups already loaded with cocoa mix. Ginny and Rebecca both had protested the idea of using prepackaged hot chocolate, but apparently Benjamin had brought it for his nieces all the way from Boston and claimed it was the best stuff he'd ever tasted.

Rebecca snagged one of the cups and swirled a plastic spoon through the mixture, combining the chocolate with the water. "Still unsure on that front. Benjamin offered me the option to continue on as the manager, but I honestly relish the idea of escaping those duties."

"What about staying on just as the baker and cook?"

She'd considered that—it would be the perfect solution. Except for one thing. "I'm not sure I could work for Benjamin."

"We'll circle back to that in a sec." Ginny sprinkled a handful of marshmallows into each cup before popping on black lids. "If you really don't have anything lined up, I'd love to have you work part-time for me."

"Seriously?" That would allow Rebecca to stay in Port Willis and work in a bakery. The part-time thing wasn't ideal, since she'd likely have to get another job as well. But perhaps it would be enough to help her get by while she focused on rebuilding her relationships with Dad and Blake. "That would be a dream. Can I think about it?"

"Of course." Ginny called to the girls, waving them over and handing each one a lidded cup of cocoa.

When Steven and Benjamin loped over to get their own drinks, Benjamin took his from Rebecca's extended hands with a wink. "My hero." His knit cap was covered in snow powder.

"Thought you could use an excuse to halt the

fight." Rebecca tsked. "Those girls are beating you pretty handily."

"I'm letting them win. Had to level the playing field." Benjamin flexed his free bicep, which looked extra silly in his puffed orange-brown jacket. "I mean, look at what they're up against."

She stroked her chin, cocked her head as she studied his arms. "What am I supposed to be looking at here?"

He chuckled and tossed back the drink, then quickly straightened and fanned at his mouth. "Ahhhh. Hot."

"Careful there, Benji-roo. Don't want to get burned."

His mouth opened as if to retort, then closed as he shook his head and apparently thought better of it. "Thanks for the chocolate, ladies."

When he left, something deflated in Rebecca's chest. Just two more days, and the banter would be over for good.

"So."

Rebecca jumped at Ginny's single word filled with so much teasing she couldn't stand to look at her friend. "What?"

"What's going on with you and my brother?"

Okay, that warranted a jerked head and widened eyes cast in Ginny's direction. "What are you talking about?"

Ginny leaned forward. "Don't act like I'm imagining something that isn't there. You and my brother … are you seeing each other?"

"No!" Had the flames leaped from the fire pit and attacked Rebecca's cheeks? Whew.

Or worse … did Ginny somehow know about the kiss?

"I thought you said you didn't want to work for him. But by the looks of things, you like him, so I guess I don't understand."

"I don't like—" Ugh. This was Ginny. Rebecca's best friend. Her only friend, really. At least for the time being. If she couldn't tell her the truth, who *could* she tell? Rebecca tugged at the ends of her hair that fell loose underneath her knit cap. "We kissed."

"What?" Now Ginny was practically hanging out of her chair. "When?"

"Two mornings ago. Just before the power went out."

"And just before you guys came over here the last time?" She clapped her hands, then pumped them in the air. "I knew it! I told Steven you both were acting strange, but he said it was all in my head. But this is great! Aw, he needs a great woman like you, Becs. And he's so good for you! You'll be so great together."

"That's the thing. There can't be an *us* together."

Ginny sat back in her chair. A breeze kicked up and blew against the fire. "Why not?"

"Uh, hullo. I live here and he doesn't."

"Sure, but plenty of couples have made that work in the short-term. You can figure it out as you go. Besides, you could move anywhere now that you're selling the inn."

"Do you think I'm the kind of woman who would chase a man?"

Ginny tapped her lip and picked up her own cup of cocoa. "I think you're the kind of woman who is strong and will chase whatever it is she wants—if she could ever decide what that is."

"What's that supposed to mean?" Rebecca followed suit and took the last cup of cocoa in hand. It warmed her fingers through her gloves.

"Just that you're afraid to want anything because you've been so disappointed in the past."

"I have good reasons for that."

"I know. You feel abandoned by your dad because he left you here. But Becs, he was just living his life. Moving on after the great loss of your mom."

She sighed. "And I don't want to begrudge him his happiness."

"I know you don't. But his decision had nothing to do with you."

"Exactly. Just like his decision to close the bakery had nothing to do with me."

Understanding lit Ginny's gaze. "People aren't perfect, Becs. They can't read minds. Maybe he thought he was doing you a favor—removing what he assumed was a burden to you and letting you be free to choose what you wanted for your own life."

Rebecca sucked in a breath. Could that really be what Dad had meant to do? Had she misjudged him and his intentions all this time?

Just one more reason why she needed to try to get over there sometime this week. Maybe even tomorrow, for Christmas, if she could manage to get a hold of him. As soon as her phone had started working again this morning, she'd tried to call, but it had gone straight to voicemail. Dad must not realize he had reception again.

Either that, or he didn't care to check on her.

She swallowed. "I hadn't thought of that. I guess I simply assumed …"

"The worst?" Ginny patted her arm, her touch tender. That of a true friend. "You tend to do that with a lot of things, Becs."

Blimey. Isn't that what she'd literally just done when thinking about Dad and his lack of a check-in call? But … Rebecca took a sip of chocolate, let the sweet warmth loosen her tongue. "It's not just Dad. It's everyone. Most especially Blake. And then there was Daniel."

"I'm still so sorry about him, Becs. That must have been terrible."

Rebecca looked away, out in the yard where everyone else had set down their cups and resumed their fight. Snowballs launched from Benjamin's spot behind the tree, and his laugh lit up the landscape as his ball struck Steven in the shoulder. Steven went down with a fake, dramatic grunt and the girls piled on top of him, giggling.

"It was. So you can see how I might have difficulty believing that anyone—especially a man—wouldn't give up on me once enough time has passed."

"I know something about that difficulty."

Of course she did. Her first husband had left her alone to "find himself"—and had ended up in another relationship while still being married to Ginny. Yet somehow, she'd managed to move forward with Steven.

"I'm not like you." Ginny was naturally predisposed to think the best of everyone. And Rebecca … well. Wasn't.

"No, but that doesn't mean it isn't possible." Her friend let out a gust of breath. "It doesn't mean that God doesn't also have amazing things for your life. That there isn't happiness right around the corner."

Could that be true? That God not only saw her, as Benjamin had suggested, but that He also had good things in store? "I just don't see how."

"Look around us. Look at what the sun is doing." Her friend shifted in her seat and pointed to the yard. The snow on the tree branches dripped a steady beat as it fell to the ground. It would take it a while to melt completely, but the process had begun.

"Would you ever have imagined, during those hours of blinding snowfall beating against our windows—the darkness, the violent wind—that the sun would shine again? That it could be like this?"

A shiver coursed up Rebecca's spine. "No. It felt like it would last forever."

"And yet …" Ginny faced Rebecca again, lifted an eyebrow. "It didn't. The storms never do. But what if you'd stayed locked inside behind your nailed up blankets? What if you hadn't ventured out today? You'd still be stuck thinking there was a storm. Still living as if one raged outside. But you didn't need to. Because the warmth has come. When we're surrounded by darkness, we just have to hold on to the hope of the light's impending arrival." She reached for Rebecca once more—and Rebecca took her hand in response. "And we need to hold onto each other too."

Tears coursed down Rebecca's cheeks and this time she didn't try to stop them. "How did you get so wise, huh?"

"Life." Offering a wry grin, Ginny squeezed Rebecca's hand. "Now come on. I think the men could use our help against my munchkins. And I've got a feeling Auntie Becs has a mean throw."

"That Auntie Becs does." Rebecca let Ginny pull her to her feet. Then she threw her arms around her friend. "Thank you, Ginny. For being my friend when no one else would. I didn't know how much I needed you. But God did. I'm so grateful that you didn't turn away even when I made it hard on you."

"Haven't I told you?" Ginny pulled back, her own eyes misty. "My favorite thing in the world is to mix two things you wouldn't think belong together—like chocolate and bacon. Amazing on their own, but when united ... well, they're magic, baby."

"You're a weird little American," Rebecca teased. "But I love you for it."

"I'm glad that's been established." Ginny wiped under her eyes, then winked—and there was something of Benjamin's mischievousness in the action. "Now, let's go toss some snowballs at my lovely daughters."

Rebecca eyed the chaos going on in the yard. Benjamin was growling as he chased Macy around a tree. "I'd rather toss them at your brother."

"By all means"—Ginny's eyes sparked—"lead the way."

Pick up, pick up ...

Dad's robotic voicemail greeting chimed in Rebecca's ear and she groaned before leaving a brief message. "Dad, I'm worried about you after that storm. Call me." Then she turned from her fireplace mantel and tossed her phone onto the couch.

"What did that phone ever do to you?" Benjamin

eased into the room carrying a small blue gift bag. What was that for?

"Just trying to reach Dad again."

"No luck?"

"Nope. Maybe he's screening my calls after all." Maybe he didn't want anything to do with her this Christmas.

"Don't lose hope, Becs. I'm sure he'll call back."

"And if he doesn't?" She squatted in front of the hearth where she'd readied the fireplace minutes ago after returning from Steven and Ginny's Christmas Eve celebration. Even though the electricity had come back on, the idea of sitting in front of the cozy fire, the bright Christmas tree, had called to her.

Rebecca struck a match and lit the kindling, then sat back on her haunches as a tiny flame grew.

"If he doesn't"—Benjamin squatted beside her— "then we'll go see him anyway."

We.

She shook her head. "I couldn't ask you to do that. You've got your family stuff tomorrow."

Christmas Day would be a flurry of activity—the roads had been cleared sometime today, so everyone would gather at Michael and Sarah's house. It was sure to be pure pandemonium, with both sides of their families, plus friends, celebrating together.

Even more reason why the quiet comfort of the B&B—her last Christmas Eve here before Benjamin purchased the place—was exactly what Rebecca needed right now.

"You aren't asking. I'm offering. Besides, we have all day. Falmouth isn't that far of a drive. I could actually do a little sightseeing while I'm here and you can play tour guide for me again." Winking, he stood and offered her a hand up, which she took. They walked to the couch and sat, a pillow between them.

It was still close enough for his citrusy scent to tiptoe toward her and take her captive. It was a wonder she ever got anything done with such a distraction around.

"Now that that's settled." Benjamin placed the gift bag on the pillow. "Merry Christmas, Becs."

"You bought me a present?"

"Well … *bought* might be a bit of a stretch. I obtained you a present."

She raised an eyebrow as she reached into the bag and pulled out several tissue-wrapped items. Opening the first, her eyes squinted. "Is this *my* spatula?"

"In my defense, we were snowed in. All the shops were closed."

Laughing, she hit him in the upper arm with it. "I like it. Serves as a weapon when I need it to."

He swiped it from her hands. "It was supposed to remind you of our baking session—and the way I stopped you from destroying that wedding cake."

"Ah." A walk down memory lane, perhaps? Her

hands trembling slightly, she opened the other items—a pen (the one he'd used to sign his initial receipt upon check-in), a sterile gauze bandage (a reminder of the burn she'd gotten and his "amazing doctoring skills"), a whisk ornament off her tree ("you didn't decorate the tree at all that night we were all here, but this one reminds me of you"), and a brochure for the Port Willis Walking Tour. He'd crossed out Marissa Johnson's name and penned in Rebecca's instead with five stars inked in above.

Staring at the items spread on the pillow in front of her, Rebecca inhaled a shaky breath. "Benjamin, this …" She swiped at a tear. "It's really sweet. You didn't have to do this."

"I wanted to."

"But I didn't get you anything."

"Sure you did." Benjamin motioned around the room. "You gave me a place to stay that didn't include a tiny yellow couch and three children who would no doubt relish crawling all over my head at six in the morning."

She snorted. "True."

He tilted his head, ran a hand behind his neck. "You gave me something else that was pretty fantastic."

"Oh yeah? What?"

"That kiss." The soft words nearly disappeared amidst the crackle of the fire, but there was no way she could miss them—spoken with awe, and a tinge of sadness too.

"Ben, that kiss was a mistake."

"Was it, though?"

"How can you say that? Of course it was."

"Why? Because of something as minor as the fact that we live on two different continents?" Benjamin waved his hand in the air as if batting away a pesky fly. "Need I remind you that my family is super wealthy? I have a private jet at my disposal and I'm not afraid to use it."

She just shook her head, fisting the tissue paper from the bag. It crinkled beneath her fingertips. "And see? That's the other thing. We're from two different worlds. You're all flashy and exciting. Handsome." Rebecca pointed a finger at his chest. "And don't go getting a big head over me saying that. It's an objective fact."

Despite her admonition, his grin rivaled the size of all of Cornwall. Then he sobered, scooting closer and reaching for her hand. "Becs, what two people in a relationship *aren't* different? I'm not saying backgrounds don't matter, but it's the way we handle them that matters more. If we communicate, if we learn from each other's differences … don't you think that differences can then become a good thing?"

He had a fair point. Also … relationship? He wanted a *relationship* with her? "So this isn't just some fling to you? A holiday romance that you'll forget about when you go home?"

"I don't do flings anymore, remember?" He wove their fingers together and set his forehead against hers. "And I couldn't forget you if I tried."

That had her caustic laugh making a return. "Why? I'm nothing special. And if you hang around me long enough, you'll see that."

"Becs." He reached a hand to her face, cupped her cheek—and suddenly, warmth enveloped her. Had she been cold before? If so, she hadn't realized it. Maybe she'd grown so accustomed to the cold—to being alone—that she'd forgotten what it was to be warm. "I was with you only a few minutes before I knew you were special. If I was privileged enough to spend even more time with you after this week, I'm positive that my first impression of you would only be cemented."

"And here my impression of you was a spoiled, arrogant jerk."

He laughed. "You aren't wrong."

"No." She nuzzled his nose with hers. "I was. You're kind and selfless and you've spent so much of your holiday making me feel better. Making me see the truth. I'm not one to admit when I'm wrong—"

At that, he laughed, and she pinched his side with her free hand. "—but I was wrong about you, Benjamin Bentley. You are everything good. And you are nothing like your father, either. Of that you can be assured."

He kissed her swiftly then, and she let him—even if they didn't have a future, they had this moment, and she couldn't find it in her to deprive either one of them. She dug her hands into that shock of thick hair at the base of his neck, and he groaned in response, pulling her closer, nearly onto his lap.

Benjamin's hands warmed her back, her hip, as his kisses deepened and slowed. How had she gone her entire life without feeling this electricity, this comfort—this spark of something that could grow roots and become love? Somehow, in a matter of days, she felt the potential in his slightest of touches. In every kiss too.

But it wasn't about the physical. Benjamin Bentley had touched the Ice Queen's heart—and it had thawed beneath his warm touch.

They pulled away simultaneously, both blinking, breathing hard. Then he fixed her with a stare. "Don't tell me you didn't feel that."

She couldn't lie. "Okay. I won't tell you."

"Becs."

"Fine." She looked away, into the fire—the endless flames that kept coming, as long as they fed it logs. "I felt it too. But ..."

"And don't tell me that we can't do that again." He gently used his thumb to turn her face back toward him. "That we can't figure something out."

A smile found her lips. "I thought being bossy was my thing."

"It is. And it's one of the first things that drew me to you."

"I don't believe that for a second."

"It's true." Benjamin traced her jaw with his fingertip and it took all her willpower not to tug him back to her for another round of kissing. "The way you took charge and bossed me around. Weren't afraid to tell me what you thought—even if that was less than favorable—it intrigued me. You're so different from any other woman I've met."

She snorted. "I'll bet. I'm not exactly a beautiful size zero with a flat stomach, hair extensions, and a wardrobe straight from Milan."

"Good, because I prefer Parisian wardrobes, anyway," Benjamin teased as he played with the ends of her hair, rubbing it between his thumb and forefinger. "And for the record, those things don't make a woman beautiful. In fact, I prefer short British bakers with a bit of a mouth on them—a very kissable mouth."

This time her cheeks warmed for a different reason. "I see." It was a completely lame response, but the man had her tongue-tied.

Thankfully, he filled in the silent gaps. "Growing up a Bentley, I never knew if a woman was truly interested in me for me or the money and power my last name brings. But you—you didn't care about that at all. And I never questioned whether you did."

"I treated you the very opposite." She rather cringed to think of that now. "I'm sorry."

"I thought you'd never apologize to anyone ever." Benjamin winked. "Besides, I love that you were real. You don't hold back—and I crave that in my life. I need it." He paused, tucking her hair behind her ear. "I need you, Becs."

Could she risk the truth? If he could be brave … "I need you too. But I just can't see how it can work between us."

"One day at a time, that's how. I'm not saying it would be easy, but don't you think it might be worth it?"

She bit her bottom lip, nodded. "Yes. But I'm going to be honest. I don't want to leave Port Willis. And if you're determined to believe that you can't leave your father's company, that you can't leave Boston, because you have to protect your sisters— who are here too—then I don't think we can have a future."

Frowning, Benjamin pulled his head back from hers. His eyes dropped to their hands, still clasped, still intertwined. After a long while, he finally spoke up again. "What if I promise to pray about it? To talk with Ginny and Sarah? Would you also pray about whether moving would be something you'd be willing to do? Not now, but someday—if we saw where this went and it got serious enough?"

It was a lot to ask of someone she'd known for a week.

And yet, she was asking it of *him*, wasn't she?

What had Ginny said earlier today? *"When we're surrounded by darkness, we just have to hold on to the hope of the light's impending arrival."* In this case, the darkness wasn't evil or a trial—it was simply the unknown. Could she, Rebecca Trengrouse, the former Ice Queen of Port Willis, choose to believe that there could be good things around the corner instead of impending doom and disaster?

Benjamin was worth that risk, wasn't he?

"Okay." She lifted their joined hands and kissed his fingers. "I'll pray about it too."

"Does this mean …?"

"It means I'm reaching out to grab your hand." She took his free hand in her free hand, so that both of his were secure in both of hers—so they anchored each other. "And I'm willing to see what comes of all this."

She lifted her chin and he angled his head downward, catching her mouth with his once more. This time, when she pulled away, she sighed. What was this feeling washing over her?

The ever-elusive peace. It must be.

"Does this mean I can call you my girlfriend?" Benjamin teased.

"Do you want to call me your girlfriend?"

"You have no idea how much."

Her cheeks heated. "Then I suppose so." She paused. "And as my boyfriend, I desperately need your help tomorrow. Because someone once told me that we were designed to need other people."

"This someone sounds wise beyond his thirty-four years."

"He likes to think so." She smiled.

He kissed her again, smooth and sound. "I'm happy to help you with anything you'd like, Girlfriend."

"Be prepared then, Boyfriend. It might be a bumpy ride."

Christmas had dawned bright and beautiful. Full of sunlight and sparkle. Full of early morning kisses and laughter as she and Benjamin had baked a casserole and pie together.

Full of hope.

But also … a tiny bit of dread.

And now here they were, after a seventy-five-kilometer drive on roads that were still a bit icy, holding said pie and casserole in carrying cases as they advanced up the walkway to a quaint house tucked away in the hills of Falmouth. The residential street was lined with vehicles—relatives and friends visiting loved ones on this most special of days.

Was it her imagination, or did someone flip open the curtains on the front windows of the house just ahead of them?

Rebecca's heart fluttered and she stopped walking, the casserole nearly toppling from her hands onto the pavement. "I don't know if I can do this."

"Just breathe, Becs. It's going to be okay."

She squinted up at him, the sun reflecting off his Ray-Bans. "What if it's not?"

He held his dish aloft. "Then at least we have pie."

Rebecca laughed. How did he always know just how to ease the tension from her shoulders? Thank goodness she wasn't alone right now. More than likely, she wouldn't be brave enough to face Dad and Melanie—and Melanie's entire family—by herself.

Especially because they didn't know to expect her.

"Let's do this." She started walking again, her boots crunching the leftover snow that had blown onto the walkway. The path wound through a tiny garden and straight on toward the traditional stone cottage wrapped in wisteria that was likely gorgeous in full bloom—Rebecca wouldn't know, as she'd only been here once, after Dad's simple wedding, when she hadn't paid much attention to her surroundings. She'd been too numb.

In some ways, that day had been worse than her mother's funeral.

Now though, she noted the details of Dad's new home. The waist-high, wrought iron gate that sat open and welcoming. The lovely wreath that looked more homemade than store-bought hanging on the cheery yellow door with segmented glass windows.

On the other side of those windows, a tiny face appeared.

Rebecca halted again. Squinted as the face disappeared just as quickly.

"What is it?" Benjamin's hand found her lower back—prepared to guide her forward or support her if she stumbled.

"I thought I saw—"

Then the door swung open and a tall man with a dark-brown beard crossed his arms over his chest.

What was he doing here? "B-Blake?"

Benjamin looked sideways at her, then back at her brother. Her brother, who lived in London and wasn't supposed to be in Cornwall for Christmas. And yet, here he was. So she hadn't imagined it— that *had* been her nephew's face at the window.

"Rebecca." Her brother nodded at her, then lifted his brow in Benjamin's direction. "And who are you?"

If Benjamin was ruffled by Blake's booming, rather aggressive tone, he didn't show it. Simply removed his hand from Rebecca's back and moved forward to offer it to Blake. "Benjamin Bentley. Rebecca's boyfriend. Nice to meet you."

Blake just stared at Benjamin's hand. "Boyfriend? Huh." Then he turned and went back inside.

The jerk.

At least he didn't slam the door, but left it wide open.

"I see welcoming introductions are a family trait."

"Ha ha." Rebecca sighed despite Benjamin's teasing tone. "Ready for that pie?"

Benjamin doubled back to join her, then leaned down to kiss her temple. "You've got this. Where's the fierce Rebecca Trengrouse who told me there was no room at the inn? That woman's a fighter."

"But I didn't come here to fight." She'd come to heal what she'd broken. What they'd all broken.

He dipped his jaw down. "No, but it might take some of that spitfire energy to get through to your brother. And time. First today. Then another day. And another. Okay?"

A breeze kicked up, blowing a mixture of sweet scents from the house.

Dad must be baking.

She nodded. "Okay." Then she advanced and stepped through the doorway into the tiny foyer that led to a cozy living room where her niece Amelia played with what looked to be a brand-new doll.

When she caught sight of Rebecca, the girl froze. A pang hit Rebecca's chest. Did Amelia not even remember her aunt?

"Aunt Rebecca?"

Oh, sweet relief. "Hi, love." Kneeling, she placed the casserole on the floor and held out her arms. When Amelia crashed into them, sending Rebecca to her rump, they both laughed. "Oh, and Amelia? Call me Auntie Becs."

"I like that." Amelia got up and ran toward what Rebecca remembered was the small stone kitchen. "Grandad! Grandma! Auntie Becs is heeeeere!"

She flinched at hearing Melanie referred to as Grandma, but what could she do? Blake's kids didn't remember Mum. They were only one and three when she died. It was nice they had a grandmother, since her sister-in-law's mom had also passed. More love to go around, right?

Benjamin helped Rebecca to her feet and she stooped to grab the casserole by the carrier's handle. Just as they headed for the kitchen, a woman in her late sixties waddled through the swinging kitchen door.

"Rebecca! What a pleasant surprise." Melanie's gray-blonde hair was pulled back in a half ponytail, and her casual look of jeans and a red sweater softened the angular features of her face. Given her open arms and sweet smile, perhaps she wasn't the heartless gold digger Rebecca had made her out to be in her mind. Not that her father had been all that well off—but still. "We didn't know you were coming." After an awkward hug, she turned to Benjamin. "And you've brought a handsome boy with you."

"Benjamin Bentley. Nice to meet you, ma'am."

Melanie chuckled. "And polite too. Let me get your father, Rebecca. Did he know you were coming and forget to tell me? He says his memory isn't that bad but just between us girls, he's full of rubbish."

Her stomach still tight, Rebecca chuckled, but it sounded forced. "I called several times yesterday but never got him."

"His phone probably died and he never got around to charging it. Thankfully, Blake and his family had already arrived before the storm—"

"He's been here this whole time?"

"Why yes, dear." Melanie tilted her head. "Your father said he called to tell you."

Oh. Maybe that's what all of those calls had been about last week.

Rebecca pinched the bridge of her nose. "Well, if you don't have enough food, we don't have to stay. I just—"

"Oh, don't be silly. We have plenty. My son and daughter should be arriving soon with their families, and then it'll get real lively in here. Make yourself comfortable. Oh!" She pointed to the casserole in Rebecca's hands and the pie in Benjamin's. "Those look lovely. Why don't you bring them into the dining room, young man? Rebecca, your father is in the kitchen."

"Oh, I don't want to bother h—"

"I've got that." Benjamin swooped in and stole her casserole, landing a swift kiss on her cheek. "And you've got this." He followed Melanie through the hall toward the dining room.

"Right." She adjusted the belt of her jacket, took a deep breath, and pushed through the door to the kitchen. Smells and a sight as familiar as breathing assailed her as soon as her feet hit the bright white tile floor.

Sugar. Flour. Baked apples.

And Dad in an apron, oven gloves on his hands as he bent at the waist to check something in the oven. He pulled out an apple crisp, set it on the stovetop, and shucked off the gloves before placing his hands on his lower back and stretching it. His eyeglasses were new, he'd trimmed his white beard closer to his jaw, and the skin on his face looked a bit more weathered than the last time she'd seen him six months ago, but this stooped seventy-something man was the same one she'd known all her life.

And yet, watching him now, there was a lightness to him she hadn't observed in years.

Maybe Melanie had done that.

"Dad?" Rebecca's voice quavered.

He started, turned, and grasped the island counter for support. "Rebecca?" His bushy eyebrows lifted and red dots marked his cheeks like he was Santa himself. "You're here."

"I am." She took a shaky step forward. "And I'm sorry it's taken me so long, Dad."

He shuffled forward and took her fully into his embrace. His shoulders shook. Was he crying?

Was she?

"Aw, my girl." Dad pulled away and pushed meaty fingers underneath his glasses to wipe at the wetness there. The recessed kitchen lighting caught his sparkling eyes. "So beautiful, just like your mum. So stubborn, just like your dad."

She laughed at that and swiped at her cheeks. "It smells good in here."

"I've been fiddling with my old apple crisp recipe. Not sure if I've got it just right." He glanced at her, his features tighter. "Don't suppose you'd like to taste it and give me some pointers?"

"Really?" When she'd been growing up, the man couldn't take a critique to save his life. And here he was actually asking for one?

He shrugged. "I've spent too many years trying to prove something. And I pushed people away because of it. Melanie's helped me see I don't have to be right all the time."

God bless Melanie.

"I'd love to swap recipe advice, Dad." She inhaled deeply, bit the inside of her cheek. "In fact, I was hoping to start getting together more." Would he be open to the idea? "Not just at the holidays."

His crooked grin told her just what he thought of it. He moved back to the counter and grabbed a few eggs out of a carton. "I'd like that. But I wouldn't want to take you away from your responsibilities at the inn." Dad cracked the eggs into the stand mixer bowl. "I know you love your work."

"That's just it." Rebecca rolled up her sleeves and joined Dad at the island, where he had flour, sugar, baking powder, and butter waiting to be measured. "I don't."

He held a cracked shell and hesitated a moment before dropping it into the rubbish bin. "But you're always so busy with it."

Too busy to visit. To take his calls.

Time for the truth—all of it.

She inhaled and grabbed the measuring cups. "Victoria sponge cake?"

He nodded.

"Alright." She measured out the sugar and dumped it into the bowl with the eggs while he did the same with the other ingredients. Her hands did the work of greasing the two cake tins while her heart figured out what to say. "The inn *does* keep me busy, but that's partly because I can't afford to hire any other employees. I've … I've failed quite miserably at it, actually. So badly I am selling it."

"What? Rebecca, no." Her dad looked like he might cry again. Wow. "I'm so sorry."

"It's actually okay." She removed her buttery hands from the tins and washed them off in the sink. "I only bought the inn as a way to bake after …" Rebecca dried her hands but continued to stare into the stone sink.

"After I closed the bakery." Dad touched her elbow and swiveled her to face him. "Ah, love. I should have asked you what you wanted. You were just off, living your life, and I didn't want you to feel you had to come back to Port Willis. But ..." He squeezed her elbow. "I should have asked."

"I thought you didn't care what I wanted. Didn't care about ..."

"About you?"

She hated to say it, but she'd promised herself she'd be honest. "Maybe."

"If that's what you've believed, I've been a poorer father than I even thought." Brow furrowed, Dad moved back to the mixing bowl and detached it, then poured the contents into the greased tins.

Grabbing a palette knife, Rebecca smoothed the tops of the batter with a few steady flicks.

Dad placed the tins into the oven and set the timer. Later, they'd create a sugar-spice syrup mixture to brush over the baked cake before adding a layer of raspberry jam and whipped cream between the two halves.

But for now, they needed to finish this conversation.

She placed a hand on his shoulder. "You weren't —aren't—a bad father."

"I pushed too hard. Pushed you away."

"Like you said—I'm stubborn. It's just as much my fault as it is yours. I assumed the worst." Rebecca grabbed a wet rag and moved it along the island counter, picking up loose crumbs.

"And I let you." He worked a hand over his bald head, frowning. "Rebecca, that bakery nearly destroyed me."

"What?" She stilled, looking up from the counter. "You loved that bakery."

"I loved it, yes. But I worried all the time. About whether it was enough to support you and Blake, your mother. My parents. During the leaner months, I thought the answer could be found in investing more time there. Really, I'd have been better off spending time with you. Before I knew it, you were gone. Off to Edinburgh, living your own life—very much away from us. Your mother blamed me, as well she should have. I know I was hard on you kids."

Had Dad ever said so many words in a row? Rebecca fisted the rag in her hand, choking back tears. This was the problem with a thawed heart. So. Much. Crying. "I don't know what to say. I was wrong too, Dad. But Ginny and Benjamin are helping me to see that things can change. I don't have to be trapped in darkness, in the past."

At that, she dropped the rag and turned to him again, hugging him. Things wouldn't be perfect— and there would still be many conversations to come —but it was a start.

A good, strong start.

"Now Ginny, I know." Dad mumbled into her hair before pulling slightly away. "But who is this Benjamin fellow?"

"Oh." She smiled. "Well, that's an interesting story. Kind of a long one too."

"As it turns out"—Dad patted one of the stools at the island—"I've got all day."

"As it turns out"—she took the seat, laughing—"so do I."

EPILOGUE

ONE YEAR LATER

"*I* still think we should add more cinnamon." Rebecca tapped the spatula against her chin, eyeing the dough she'd rolled out on the inn's kitchen island. "They're cinnamon rolls, after all."

"It's perfect. Too much cinnamon makes the eyes water." Dad frowned. "I've always said that."

Rebecca took a step toward him. A year may have passed—their relationship better than ever before—but he still liked to argue with her. "And *I* say—"

"You're both wrong." Ginny breezed into the kitchen. "We need less cinnamon, not more."

"Should we make a contest out of it?" Dad rubbed his hands together, glee in his gaze. "I'm catching up to you both in this crazy point system you've got going on."

Rebecca waggled her eyebrows. "How about we

all make some and let our guests decide which is best?" It was the day before Christmas Eve and they had a full house at the inn, including Dad and Melanie, who were spending the holidays in Port Willis this year. Blake and Shelby would be down sometime today with their kiddos. Rebecca had teased Blake that if he got there too late, he'd miss all the fun, but he'd just rolled his eyes over the Face-Time video and said he'd take his chances.

No, things weren't perfect between them yet. Probably never would be.

But they were good.

"That is an excellent idea." Ginny grinned. "But unfortunately, I've got a few things left to do at the bakery before we close up for the holiday weekend. Besides, your boss is about to arrive. Aren't you leaving to go pick him up soon? That's why I really came over here—to see if you'd left."

Rebecca checked the clock over the door. "Blimey. The morning got away from me. Dad, you were supposed to remind me when it was time for me to leave."

"Was I?" He hmmed. "Go, go, then. Guess I'll just have to finish up these cinnamon rolls without you." He sounded entirely too pleased at the prospect.

"Just don't ruin them, old man."

He chuckled, a deep baritone that had become one of her favorite sounds. "I was making these before you were born, you know. And everyone loves my recipe."

"Almost everyone." Rebecca winked before removing her apron and kissing him on the cheek. "Thanks for helping in here today while Charlotte's out of town." Since Benjamin had taken over the inn last year, he'd made quite a few changes, including hiring an entire staff to run the place. Charlotte now split her time between the bakery and the inn, where she normally ran the housekeeping services. Rebecca had been filling in while she was away.

Event planner Georgiana worked as a contractor whenever the inn held a wedding or other event— which, thanks to Benjamin's robust social media and marketing plan, was nearly every week now.

Luke had left the bookstore and worked full-time as the inn's manager. Sophia still hadn't stopped giving Benjamin grief over stealing her best employee, but she'd found a nice college student of William's to help out on the days Emily and Edward didn't have school and Kathryn wasn't with her childminder.

And Rebecca? Well, she had the best gig of all. Benjamin had begged her to stay on as the inn's baker and chef, and they'd expanded to serving all three meals a day to their guests—not just breakfast.

It was, in fact, a dream.

The only part that wasn't dreamlike was the fact her boyfriend still lived in Boston. They'd both done their share of traveling back and forth this last year. It wasn't sustainable—they both knew it. But Rebecca was too in love to break up with him. That man had made her into a simpering fool and she didn't even care in the slightest.

She'd be a fool for Benjamin Bentley any day.

But leave Port Willis? Could she do that? Whenever she thought about how this place she'd always called home had, for the first time in forever, actually felt like it—her insides hurt. She couldn't give it up.

And yet, she couldn't give up Benjamin either.

She held in a sigh. They had a lot to talk about during this visit. But first, she'd do her best to forget all that and simply enjoy time with her friends and family.

"I'm happy to help out." Dad's voice brought her back to reality—and the fact she needed to scurry out of there if she was going to make it to the airport in time to pick up Benjamin. "What else is an old, retired goat like me going to do?"

"You're only as old as you feel, Dad. Bye, Gin! Thanks for reminding me to go get your brother." Rebecca whisked through the door into the dining room, where a family from Scotland sat around the table drinking cocoa and playing cards. They waved hello and she responded with a smile before snagging her purse and jacket by the reception desk where Luke and Georgiana stood going over details for some upcoming event—and looking quite cozy doing it, even if they insisted they were only friends. The pair didn't even look up to say goodbye to Rebecca.

Slipping on her jacket, Rebecca made her way into the fading sunlight. So far, there had only been a very light sprinkling of snow and it had turned to muddy slush beneath car tires and boots, but bits of it sparkled beneath the light of the lampposts that lined the street. A few shoppers loaded with bags passed her on one side as she hurried up High Street to the car park where she kept her vehicle.

As she moved past the children's playground and gazebo, her eyes caught on the spot near the bluff where she'd first started to open her heart to Benjamin on the tour of Port Willis she'd given him a year ago. It stood just beyond the village Christmas tree, which had been decorated and lit last weekend in the village-wide Winter Walk that culminated in the lighting ceremony.

In past years, she'd attended purely as a concession to Ginny who had dragged her there. But this year, she'd gone willingly, stringing her arms through Jessie's and Lila's as they sang carols.

And she'd missed Benjamin the whole time.

He should have been there. He belonged here as much as she did. He—

She squinted at the tree again. Someone stood in front of it.

Not just someone. How—

But she didn't care how. Rebecca sprinted across the expanse of grass that stood between her and the tree.

Between her and her love.

The man turned and she barely caught a glimpse of that familiar grin as she crashed her body into his, nearly taking him down. "Hey, Becs."

"Benjamin! What"—she kissed him hard on the mouth—"are you doing here? I was on my way to come to get you."

"I caught an earlier flight." He held her around the waist and brought his lips to hers again. His stubble rubbed against her cheeks, but she didn't mind in the least as she melted into him. "Your dad helped me delay you."

"You used my own father as an accomplice against me?" She mock-glared at him. "How dare you."

"Not *against* you, love." The wind blew the ends of his scarf back. "I just thought it would be fun."

"Then why did you stop here at the park instead of coming straight to me?"

"Had to make my first-ever contribution to the tree since I didn't come prepared last year. It's just a lucky coincidence that you happened to catch me— because otherwise, I was going to have to bring you back to see it."

Turning out of his arms, Rebecca studied the tree.

She reached out to touch a purple racecar ornament. Some child's contribution, no doubt—or that of an adult with a kid's heart. "Which one's yours?" Her eyes followed the branches, spanning up and outward, reaching toward her as if to grasp her hand.

Benjamin leaned down, pressing his nose into her hair, his lips blowing warm breath against her ear. "Guess."

A year together and the man still made her shiver.

She elbowed him lightly in the stomach. "There are hundreds if not a thousand ornaments here. How am I to find yours?"

"I know you like a challenge." His eyes glinted a tease in the waning light and Rebecca pursed her lips.

Hmmm. "Challenge accepted." Angels and penguins, beloved Christmas movie characters like Rudolph and the Grinch, dinosaurs in Santa hats, snow globes and snowmen. Nothing that screamed *Benjamin* or what was important to him.

Rebecca rubbed her hands together and exhaled, her breath a puff of white thanks to the dipping temperature. "Give me a hint or we'll be here all night."

"Giving up already?"

"A hint does *not* mean I'm giving up."

"Hmm."

"It doesn't!"

He laughed at the indignation in her tone. "Alright, alright." Then he pointed a little to the right and, thankfully, at her eye level. "It's somewhere in this general vicinity."

She pushed him out of the way to make room to peruse, and he reached his arms around her from behind, setting his chin on top of her head. She should protest the distraction, but their month-long separation had been much too lengthy. And they were set to endure another one when he had to go back home in just a few days. How could they keep going like th—

No. She wouldn't dwell on that now. Rebecca snuggled back against him and continued to let her eyes wander the branches.

And just when she was about to concede her defeat—which showed lots of personal growth over the last year, didn't it?—her gaze snagged on the ornament that had to be Benjamin's.

Easing out of his arms, she stepped forward and went up on her tiptoes to reach for the ornament. About the size of her palm, it was an exact replica of the bed and breakfast—which they'd renamed and rebranded as Rebecca's Holiday Inn, "where every day is a holiday."

There were the dormer windows. The red door that matched the berries on the wreaths and small porch trees. The chimney with puffs of smoke twirling into the inky sky.

"Where did you get this made?" She stroked the ornament's painted face with her gloved finger. The detail was exquisite.

"I have a friend who makes custom ornaments."

"Well, it's beautiful. And we need one for the inn's tree. Please tell me you got two."

"This one is unique, I'm afraid. Especially because of what's inside."

Inside? She examined the ornament more closely, turning it over. Sure enough, the bottom part of the inn appeared to pop open. She tried the clasp but it didn't budge. Rebecca's nose scrunched and she turned to face Benjamin behind her. "Benj—"

She froze. The crazy man was kneeling in the snow. Why was he—

Wait.

He was on one knee.

And she was holding an ornament with a hidden compartment.

Blimey.

"There it is." Benjamin's eyes laughed, probably at how long it had taken her to put two and two together. "Open it, Becs."

"I don't…" Her hands shook. "I can't."

His face went slack. "Oh."

She was making a mess of this, wasn't she? "I

don't mean I can't marry you—because I'm assuming you're about to ask me."

"So many assumptions."

"I mean I can't open it. It's stuck."

His mouth in a teasing slant, he took the ornament from her outstretched hand and, with no effort at all, popped it open.

"I loosened it for you." Rebecca bent forward and plucked a ring from the center of the open ornament. It was white gold, the diamond a perfect square with tiny clusters of other diamonds surrounding it. And it stole her breath, plain and simple.

"About to get engaged and you're still arguing with me."

Somehow, Benjamin always had a way of bringing her back to reality—back to herself. "Now who's making the assumptions?" Rebecca held back the grin threatening to break loose. "I might not say yes."

"Maybe I shouldn't ask, then …"

"Oh, get on with it already." She bounced on her tiptoes—and not just because it was getting chillier by the moment.

"There's the bossy woman I know and love." Benjamin tipped his head to the side before holding out his hand, palm outstretched. "Can I get that back? Trying to propose over here."

She set it carefully in the center of his hand. "And you're really slow at it too."

"Says the person here whose knee isn't currently soaked through and freezing."

Rebecca giggled, then made a "let's get on with it" hand motion. Was this real? Was the man she loved about to ask her to marry him? To—

Wait. To what?

To move to Boston?

Just what would she be agreeing to?

"Ben …"

"Rebecca—"

They spoke simultaneously. His eyebrows raised. "What's wrong?"

She cleared her throat. "How is this going to work? I … I'm not sure about leaving Port Willis. Not now, when I have everything I want—everything but you, here with me. But—" Could she really say the words? Could she take the next step even though she couldn't see a way forward, a way for them to both be happy?

Could she trust that God saw, that He knew, even if she didn't—and that was okay?

Yes. The word tumbled and spun through the air on the breeze, as sure and peace-filled as a whisper.

"But"—she continued—"I will, if that's what it takes to be with you. Because I don't know a lot in this life, but I know that our two lonely hearts were meant to find each other."

Benjamin's hand closed around the ring and he stood in a flash, kissing her with fierce abandon. When he pulled back, his finger traced her jaw. "First of all, Rebecca Trengrouse, I never thought I'd see the day when you would spout cheesy romance at me."

"It's your fault." She hooked her hands around his neck. "You ruined my plan."

"And what plan was that?"

"I told you … I never planned to fall in love."

"And I told you that's not something you can plan."

"Still, I was determined to avoid it. But you were just too darn persistent. So like I said. It's all your fault."

The evening had fully arrived and the tiny lights on the tree winked at them as Benjamin settled one hand on her hip and held up the ring in front of her face with the other. "Now, as I was saying—"

"What's *second of all?*" At his confused look, she nudged his nose against hers. And yes, he probably thought she was the most annoying woman on the planet, but really—he should have known her well enough by now. She was, as they said, like a dog with a bone. "You said *first of all*. That means there must be a *second of all*."

"Ah." He kissed her nose, her cheeks, her jaw before landing his mouth on hers. "*Second of all*, I know you're worried about the future. But I want you to know that I've quit my job and—"

"You what?" She jerked back, but he held her fast. "I didn't ask you to do that." Not really, even if she'd wished it a thousand times.

"And you'll never know what that means to me. Leaving my dad's company had to be my choice. But I've done a lot of soul-searching this last year, and with all the back and forth, I've realized something—this is home. Because you're here. My sisters are here. And I've actually got a real knack for turning around floundering small businesses like the inn."

"*Floundering* sounds a bit harsh, don't you think?" She smiled and batted her eyes.

"Anyway"—he smiled as he emphasized the word—"I want to do that for a living, and I can do that here in England just as well as I do in Boston. Which means that I'm moving here, effective immediately."

"Wait. Seriously?"

"Well, that is, if you'll agree to my proposal."

"You're proposing?" Her grin widened.

"If you'll ever let me, you exasperating woman."

She stepped back from his embrace and peeled off her left glove. Held out her hand. "I'm glad you've finally recognized who's really in charge here."

"I've always known that." His eyes sparkled with that mischief she so well loved. "Now, can I get on with the proposal, please?"

"I suppose I'll allow it."

"Good." Benjamin removed his glove too, so that when he took her hand, the warmth of his skin seeped into hers. "Before I met you, I'd seen love at work in other people's lives. I'd seen it make Ginny more confident. It made Sarah braver. It made Kara vulnerable. Warren, more independent. But I didn't know if it could do that for me. To be honest, I didn't even know if love could exist for me after all the ways I'd screwed up. All the ways I'd failed."

She squeezed his hand. Her eyes already burned at his sweet words—words she never thought she'd hear from someone until he'd walked into her life and ruined all her plans.

"Rebecca Trengrouse, you have helped me to see that I can be whoever I want to be. I'm not automatically destined to be like my father. I don't need to be everyone else's savior. That's what God is for. You make me want to be a better man—a good husband, one who spends all of my days seeing you and mining the depths of who you are for the treasures God has created in you."

Gah. Yeah, there came the tears. A gushing torrent, but she blinked so her eyes didn't miss a thing—didn't miss a moment of this memory they were making.

"So Rebecca—Becs—will you please, please put me out of my misery and marry me?"

She opened her mouth to reply, but a hiccup fell out instead. All she could do was nod and wiggle her frozen fingers at him. He slipped the ring on and kissed her soundly.

And quite thoroughly too.

Then he set his forehead against hers. "Does this mean I can call you my fiancée?"

She smiled. "Do you *want* to call me your fiancée?"

"Not as much as I want to call you my wife," he whispered. "Please don't make me wait too long."

"Good things come to those who wait," she whispered back, teasing him.

And of course—OF COURSE—the sky decided that it was the perfect moment to agree. Either that, or God was sending them an early wedding gift.

Because a flurry of snow began to fall at that very moment.

Benjamin grinned and dipped, his lips hovering just above her mouth. "I've waited for you my whole life. I think I've been patient enough."

Hmmm. "You're right."

He reared back in mock surprise. "Can I get that in writing?"

"Not on your life."

Benjamin chuckled. "Never change, Becs."

"Only for the better, I hope."

"Amen."

Then his mouth claimed hers and she caught a glimpse of the road winding ahead of them, lit by the gentle flame of the One who saw—and loved—them both.

It wasn't perfectly straight. There were dips and valleys. Mountains too.

But perfection was overrated, anyway.

I hope you enjoyed Benjamin and Rebecca's story! I had so much fun with the banter and romance in this one. I suppose that's no surprise, since I've been busy writing sweet romantic comedies under the pen name Kristin Canary!

Can't get enough of Port Willis? Don't forget to check out Port Willis Romance Books 1-3, starting with *Like a Winter Snow*!

*And **if you want more small town romance** from me, check out my Walker Beach Romance series, starting with All of You, Always. Read on for a sneak peek...*

So this was Walker Beach.

A place that would finally help Bella Moody assemble the puzzle of her past—*if* she did her job.

Bella angled her car down the Main Street loop. Flashes of the Pacific Ocean to her left reflected the sun's rays between the downtown buildings, which were painted in cheery yellows, robin blues, and coral pinks. Other than its location in California, Walker Beach was nothing like Bella's home in Los Angeles.

The town had character—she'd give it that. But despite the fact Mom had called the little tourist town a "summer hotspot," the streets didn't seem overly crowded, even on a Friday afternoon in July. Probably had something to do with the earthquake last weekend.

The earthquake that had finally given Moody Development an edge.

Before she could blink, Bella had cruised by an art gallery, City Hall, a bookstore, and a smattering of restaurants. After passing a small public parking lot, she hit the northern part of town, which finally showed evidence of the earthquake.

Bella slowed her car and rolled down her windows to take in the damage, including a few downed roofs, some broken front windows, and siding that hadn't fared well against the force. From the reports she'd read, the tremor had only registered a 6.5 on the Richter scale, with no loss of lives but damage to several homes in the hills and about ten businesses along Main Street.

Including her destination—the Iridescent Inn.

She came to a crosswalk and stopped for a young pigtailed girl with a thirty-something couple. The girl turned to the adults and reached for them. "Mama! Daddy! Swing me!"

Laughing, they each took a hand and swung her between them as they crossed the road.

Bella rubbed a hand over her heart. That child didn't know how lucky she was. Not only to have a mom *and* a dad in her life but also to have the security of their love.

She rolled her windows back up. No sense in waxing sentimental about what had never been—at least for her. But the perfect picture in front of Bella reinforced her determination to find out what she'd always longed to know. Maybe even to change her future.

If only there were another way to obtain the information she sought.

Shaking loose of the grim thought, Bella hightailed it through the rest of town, past a huge community park situated along the beach, and about a mile outside of Walker Beach until she reached her destination. The Iridescent Inn sat on a bluff with a path that led down to a private beach.

Mom had chosen well. Now it was up to Bella to seal the deal.

She swallowed past her dry throat. Pulling into the parking lot, Bella climbed from her Lexus sedan. Only a single beat-up Ford pickup truck accompanied her car.

The breeze coming up from the ocean whipped Bella's brown ombre hair across her face as she maneuvered to her trunk and pulled a travel-sized suitcase from inside it. Bella headed toward the adorable inn. Of course, it was no Waldorf Astoria in Beverly Hills, but its Victorian-style wraparound porch and dormer windows cast it in the same cozy light as the rest of the town.

Bella's Louboutins crunched over the gravel parking lot as she approached the front door. From here, she couldn't make out any damage to the inn, but Mom's source had assured them that the hundred-year-old building hadn't escaped without a rather significant scratch. Bella reached for the knob on the red front door, but it held fast.

After knocking on the door without a reply, she whipped out her cell phone then looked up the inn's number and dialed. Her legs ached as she shifted from foot to foot, the result of being crammed into the car for nearly five hours—thank you, endless LA traffic.

Great. No answer.

The ground beneath her feet rumbled. Bella shoved her phone into her purse and held as steady as possible while riding out the aftershock, which only lasted thirty seconds. She would probably experience hundreds of little quakes while here.

A crash cracked through the air, and Bella's heart stuttered as she maneuvered into a defensive position despite the pencil skirt that restricted her movement. But other than a few cars passing on the street just beyond the inn, no one was anywhere to be seen. Bella turned her ear to the wind. Another collision, this one a bit quieter, came from the backside of the building, so she walked that way, suitcase in tow.

As she rounded the inn, she nearly gasped at the view—at the whiff of briny spray in the air that spoke of fun and relaxation in the sun. Of retreats and vacation. Of the West Coast at its finest.

No wonder Mom was willing to pay through the

nose for this property. When combined with the two B&Bs that Moody Development had already bought on either side of the Iridescent Inn, this location would make for a beautiful—and profitable—new resort.

Once Bella convinced Ben Baker to sell.

She let herself through the wrought-iron gate that led from a walled-in courtyard down toward the beach. Trees provided a lot of shade, and a stone fountain nearby gave a pleasant ambience despite the fact no water trickled down its face.

But that's where the charm gave way to destruction. From this side of the inn, the significant scratch —or scratches, rather—became obvious. The entire northwestern wing of the Iridescent Inn had visible damage, with a hole in the northern part of its roof, cracks in the western blue clapboard siding, and scattered roof tiles and wood that lay strewn below.

She walked closer, her eyes moving along the house, taking in every casualty. The poor old inn had met its match in the earthquake.

As she stood next to a partially collapsed winding staircase that led to a damaged upper-story deck, a pang of sympathy curled around Bella's heart—even though all this *was* to her advantage.

The ground began to shake again as nature showed off with another aftershock. A large dangling piece of the staircase's railing cracked and plummeted through the air toward Bella.

"Watch out!"

Before she could even shriek, a flash of movement crossed her path as someone knocked into her with a grunt, felling her breath. Bella rolled a few times until she landed on her back. Taking in a few gulps of air, she cringed at something beneath her and pulled out a sharp rock that she tossed aside.

"Are you hurt?"

Bella turned her head to find a man sitting next to her, groaning as he rubbed his head before looking her way.

She peered up into warm chocolate eyes and a handsome tan face. Her tongue grew heavy. "No."

Scratch that. Her knees and elbows pulsed with a raw pain like the first time she'd ridden a bike without training wheels at the age of seven. Down the hill she had flown, and when she'd reached the bottom, onto the asphalt she had splayed. As usual, Mom hadn't been there. "Nothing feels broken at least."

"That's good." The man peeled thick work gloves from his hands as he bent toward her, squinting, examining, his eyebrows knit together. "Your knees are scraped up, but it's nothing a good cleaning and some BAND-AIDs won't fix."

"Guess I won't be wearing my favorite little black dress anytime soon." Bella forced a chuckle at her bad joke. She wouldn't need to wear something fancy if she were here for any length of time.

Not that she intended to be—though if Mr. Baker turned out to be as obstinate toward Bella as he'd been toward Mom, well, who knew how long she'd be stuck in the middle of nowhere.

"Can you sit?" Her rescuer watched Bella, something deep and assessing in his gaze.

Bella's stomach roiled at the scrutiny as her mother's warning came to mind. *"You'll have to be on your toes at all times."*

Right. She needed to focus. This minor incident couldn't endanger her mission, however conflicted she was about it.

"I think so."

"Here. Let me help you." He offered his hand. His white long-sleeved T-shirt pulled against his broad chest.

"Thanks." Bella slipped her fingers inside his, nearly pulling away at the shock his touch rendered, like the static electricity that always clung to the end of a slide and zapped kids when they least expected it.

After getting her upright, the guy let go of her hand and ran his fingers through his blondish-brown crew cut. "I'm really sorry about this."

She glanced down at her injuries and nearly cried out. The heel of her left Louboutin pump had snapped off and laid lifeless on the dirty ground, a victim of the aftershock and subsequent fall. Mom had better reimburse that as a business expense.

"It's not your fault. I shouldn't have been standing so close to the staircase."

"I was out here cleaning up when I saw you." A yellow hard hat lay discarded upside down on the other side of him. Mr. Baker must have hired him to clear the debris from the earthquake damage. "Another second or two and that loose railing would have creamed you."

"Instead, you got the privilege." Her fingers clenched as the words she'd intended to be a joke released in a stiff tone.

He hesitated. "I was just trying to help."

"Oh, no. Yeah." Why were her words getting all jumbled in her delivery? She took a breath and tried again. "I'm grateful. Really."

"Well . . . I'll go fetch the first aid kit." Again the man studied her, almost as if he knew something about her.

I hope not. Shivering, Bella stood, wincing at an ache in her backside. "That's OK." She needed to get checked in, hopefully before meeting the inn's owner. First impressions were everything in Bella's world, and she was sure they mattered even outside of the big city. "I'll come with you." She located her suitcase a few feet away.

His eyes narrowed for a moment. "Are you . . ." He massaged his jaw for a moment then shook his head and headed toward the front of the hotel.

Well, that was strange. She followed him, hobbling on her broken heel.

He snuck a hand into the pockets of his Dickies and emerged with a key that he used to open the door before pushing his way inside. Huh. Maybe he was more than a contractor hired to fix the earthquake damage.

The inside of the inn exuded just as much charm as the outside, and from here Bella wouldn't have even known of the damage along its northwestern facade. Real wood floors led to a quaint reception desk that welcomed guests into the ten-by-ten foyer. Behind it, a staircase ascended to a second level. If memory served from her brief moments perusing the website, the twenty-room inn had a small lobby at the top of the stairs and rooms on both floors. The deck she'd seen from the courtyard in the back met up with the lobby and provided guests with a gorgeous view of the ocean and beach below.

Speaking of other guests, where were they?

Bella cleared her throat. "I'm guessing all that debris is from the earthquake?"

"Yeah, and things are a mess. Most of the town was spared, but a few of us were hit hard. It could have been worse." The workman squatted behind the reception desk and started digging, finally emerging with a box of bandages and a tube of what she assumed was antibiotic ointment.

"Here you go." He shoved the stuff into her hands

and leaned back against the desk, chiseled arms folded over his chest. The scent of clean soap lingered in the space between them.

"Thanks." The edges of the BAND-AID wrappers crinkled in her fingers. She itched to get out of her dusty clothes, but this was a prime opportunity to gather intel. And even though her assignment left a sour taste in her mouth, that's why she was here after all. "Were there any guests staying at the inn when the earthquake struck?"

Something ticked in the man's jaw. "Thankfully not." His arms tightened, emphasizing his biceps even more. "Speaking of guests, I notice you have a suitcase with you, but I don't have any reservations in my system for today. Can I ask what you were doing in my courtyard?"

His system? *His* courtyard? Bella blinked. "Are you the owner?"

"Yep. Ben Baker, at your service."

"Oh." She couldn't hold back her grimace. So much for first impressions. "Nice to meet you."

"And you are?"

She couldn't miss how steel rimmed his tone. Something about his clear distrust weakened her muscles. But why should she care what he thought? She didn't know him. And Bella Moody was used to playing ball with much more intimidating businessmen than Ben Baker.

Of course, in this case, playing ball meant using

stealth. Getting the inside scoop. Winning him over so she could discover his weaknesses and take what she wanted.

Well, what Mom wanted.

But if Bella succeeded, her mother would finally give Bella what *she* wanted. The one thing she wanted more than anything. The thing *only* Mom could give.

Information.

She stepped forward, her legs wobbly—and not just because of her missing heel. Guess she cared what he thought after all.

"Bella M—" Yikes, she'd almost ruined everything with one word. She needed to stick with her plan if things weren't going to fall apart in the first five minutes. More than they already had, anyway. "Bella Miranda."

At least she wasn't lying. Miranda was her middle name.

It was a small consolation.

Stay focused. Remember why you're really here. Let that guide you.

"And what are you doing in town?"

"I'm here on a personal errand." She glanced at her suitcase. "And no, I don't have a reservation, but I was hoping you'd have space for me."

He lifted off the desk, his arms falling to his sides. "You really want to stay here after nearly being taken out by that railing?"

"Is it safe on the inside?" If not, she'd have to find somewhere else in town to stay, some other way to get to know Ben. The whole plan would go much more smoothly if she could be here.

"The building inspector finally came today and gave me the all-clear to enter. Only half of the inn is damaged. If you stay away from the courtyard and don't go north of the lobby, you should be OK." The pinched look on his face relayed his resignation. "But I'd need you to sign a waiver stating that you understand the risks."

"All right."

He waited for a beat. "All right as in . . ."

"I'll stay."

Was that a kindling of hope smoldering in Ben's eyes? It was there and gone so quickly that maybe she'd imagined it. "We do, in fact, have a few vacancies right now." He rounded the desk and snagged the computer mouse. "Do you want one queen or two twins?"

"One queen is fine."

"And how long do you want to stay?"

"Can we just start with a week? I'll let you know if I need to stay longer."

Ben glanced up. "You don't know how long you'll be here?"

"I'm not sure when my business will be concluded." And wasn't that the truth? "One more thing. I'd like to pay in cash, if that's all right."

Ben's eyebrows lifted. "We normally require a credit card on file in case there are damages."

She couldn't give him a credit card with her real last name on it, now could she? Her stomach twisted at the need for such deceit, but she pushed the uneasiness aside. "I'm happy to pay for a week at a time up-front, plus I can give you a deposit in case there are damages. Not that I plan to damage anything."

He studied her for a moment, probably weighing whether she'd walk out if he refused. Finally, he nodded. "You're not the first person to come to Walker Beach looking for anonymity. Two hundred should cover the deposit, which will be refunded when you check out as long as nothing's damaged."

"Sounds great."

He took her cash then worked to check her in.

So far, except for his penetrating gazes and slightly bristly manner, he'd been all business—an admirable quality, actually, considering how often guys hit on Bella when she was doing the most mundane of tasks like grocery shopping or working out at the gym. But this was one instance where a chatty demeanor would have been helpful.

Because everything was riding on getting Ben to like her.

And people didn't open up to those they didn't like, so to succeed here, she needed to gain his trust.

At least, that's what Mom had said before she'd sent Bella off on this mission.

Hating herself more than a little and feeling as fake as a metal tree at Christmas, Bella cocked a hip and propped an arm on the desk. While Ben clicked around on the screen, she pointed to a framed photo a few inches away that showed a huge group of people smiling at the camera. "Is that your family?"

Not looking up, he nodded. "Yep. Family reunion last year."

She peered closer and finally found Ben in the upper left corner, his arm slung around a tall blond girl with similar features. "Who's that?"

He looked up with a frown and something like irritation in his eyes. "My sister, Ashley."

What would it be like to have a real family—not just a mom who was more a boss than anything?

Maybe, at the end of all this, Bella would finally know.

Keep him talking. Right. "So, what's there to do around here?"

A printer whirred to life behind Ben. He snagged some papers and turned, handing them to Bella along with a pen. "Tons. Of course, there's surfing, kayaking, and other water sports. If you need any equipment or want to take a tour, my cousin Cameron manages a rental shop and could set up something for you. There's also a lot of shopping downtown if antiques, art galleries, and specialty shops are your thing."

She flourished her signature across the safety waiver and contract detailing the security deposit regulations. "Any good places to eat?"

"My personal favorites are Froggies Pizza and the Frosted Cake."

Her stomach rumbled to life at the suggestions. The tiny pack of airplane peanuts she'd found at the bottom of her purse hardly sufficed for a meal, but that's all she'd eaten since breakfast. "Those sound amazing." She angled her head and pushed her lips into a grin that felt anything but natural. "Would you happen to be available to join me?"

Ben stiffened. "Can't. The earthquake put me behind on everything."

Great. The prickly owner clearly wanted nothing to do with her—except to take her money, of course. What now? "Rain check, maybe?"

"I'm really slammed." He averted his eyes and slid a key card against the desk's polished surface. "Your room is just upstairs and down the south hallway. Third door on the left. If you need anything, I'll be in my office, which is just around the corner off the kitchen."

Bella snatched the key card and tried for a casual tone. "Sounds good. Thanks."

She strode toward the staircase, wincing at the tightened skin on her kneecaps. Maybe this *was* more like that first time riding a bike than she'd realized, with the hill too steep and Bella too bullheaded to see she shouldn't attempt it.

But just like that day twenty years ago, she was going to keep dragging her bike all the way to the top. She was going to have to change her strategy, but she'd try again and again until she finally mastered it.

No matter her own reservations, she *would* get Ben Baker to agree to sell his inn to her mom. It didn't matter that Mom had been trying for at least six months. Bella could accomplish what no one else could simply because she had more riding on this than anyone else.

Sure, Mom wanted the deal so she could finally build the resort she'd been dreaming of. The place would be a gold mine.

But Bella wanted something more than money. She and her mom had come from poverty, and poverty could find them again at any time. But a family—well, families were forever. And Bella wanted to know if she had one out there, somewhere.

So, bring on the hill because Bella Moody would do just about anything to find out who her father was and whether he'd been survived by any family when he'd died twenty-seven years ago.

❄

Numbers were Ben Baker's enemy.

Especially when they were red. Very, very red.

Ben scrubbed a hand across his face and leaned back in his office chair as the spreadsheet swam in front of him on the screen. Grandpa would roll over in his grave if he could see how badly Ben was botching his legacy.

His one saving grace would be the insurance money from the earthquake, which he hoped he would get an update on by Monday. He'd likely have to do most of the repairs himself—and maybe he'd snag his buddy Evan or a few of his cousins to help out—but that would leave extra money on the table to pay off some of his debts.

Like the mortgage he'd defaulted on three months ago.

But if the four cancellations that had just come in this afternoon and the numbers bleeding on the screen indicated what was to come, the Iridescent Inn was in dire trouble.

Ugh. He needed a break.

Easing away from the desk, Ben strode to his office door then into the hallway and up the stairs toward the lobby, where the world's most comfortable couches awaited him. Maybe a little time stretched out on one of those bad boys would refresh him enough to come up with a plan.

But as he reached the top of the stairs and pivoted toward the pair of deep green couches ringing the stone fireplace against the south wall, Ben halted.

There sat the woman who had checked in only a few hours ago, a large pizza box on the scratched oak coffee table in front of her along with a stack of plates and napkins. She glanced up at his arrival. "Oh. Hi. I hope it's OK I'm in here."

Earlier she'd been all business in that skirt that had hugged her curvy lower half and heels that had looked painful to walk in. Now she looked much more relaxed—though somehow still classy—in black yoga pants and a flowy blue shirt that brought out the chocolate brown of her eyes.

The same eyes that had drawn him in earlier when he'd "rescued" her in the courtyard. Ben had imagined something mysterious and vulnerable in their depths. Probably he'd just whacked his head harder than he'd thought.

"Of course it's OK." His voice came out gruffer than he'd intended. He attempted to soften his tone. "I didn't mean to intrude."

"You're not. I was just thinking it would be nice to have some company. And there's plenty of food." The woman—Bella, if he remembered correctly— waved her hand toward the Froggies pizza box. Even from here the smell of hot cheese and his uncle's secret pizza sauce tantalized his senses. "Would you like to join me?"

"Thanks for the offer, but I have a ton of work to

do." He really did but that wasn't his prime motivation for turning her down. "And I'm not hungry." Neither was that.

His stomach chose that moment to betray him. It rumbled like a train coming into the station.

The woman quirked an eyebrow. "Of course you're not."

When she opened the lid of the box, Ben couldn't help but lean forward at the sight of pepperoni and sausage spread generously across the top of the pizza. "I guess I'll have some." He reached into his back pocket, snagged his wallet, and pulled out a ten, which he tossed next to her onto the couch. "That should cover my half."

"Not necessary. It's my treat." Bella took a piece of pizza from the box, slid it onto a plate, and held it out for Ben. "Here."

Ben accepted the plate then shifted on his feet. "Thanks. But seriously, keep the money." On the off chance she was trying to make this into some sort of date, maybe his insistence would make it clear he was not interested. "I should go back to my office."

Bella settled back against the couch. "I understand." Her tone remained crisp, professional. "Hope you get a lot done." Moving her gaze to the unlit fireplace, she bit into the pizza and chewed.

Aw, man. Something about the interaction wasn't sitting right with him. His mom's voice yapping at him to treat women well—dumb chivalry—resounded in his mind, and it seemed wrong to leave Bella to eat here alone in a town where she might not know anyone.

And all because he was, what? Afraid she was flirting with him? Most likely she was just a nice person and offering a hungry guy some food.

Not all women were conniving like Elena.

Besides, he didn't want to insult the one paying customer willing to stay in an inn falling down around her ears. "All right. I can stay for a few minutes." Then he'd get out of there and back to the safety of his office. Ben slid onto the other couch and bit into the pizza but didn't taste a thing.

The clock on the mantel ticked. Loudly.

After several minutes of silence, Bella finished her pizza. Once she'd placed the plate on the coffee table, she wiped her lips with a napkin. "That was really good. Thanks for the recommendation."

Maybe she'd go back to her room now.

But nope. She stayed put.

Ben suppressed a sigh. "I'll pass along the compliment to my uncle and aunt. Froggies is their restaurant."

"Please do. I think I met another Baker when I was out, just before I grabbed the pizza. The owner of Serene Art? Any relation?"

"My aunt Jules."

Bella crossed her legs. "Your aunt? She looked really young."

"She's forty-two." Only ten years older than him. His first babysitter.

"It sounds like you have a lot of family in town."

"Yeah. My dad has four siblings, and they're all here."

She tilted her head. "Are all of them business owners?"

"Yep."

"Wait, seriously?"

Was her response disbelief or awe? Or maybe a mix of both. So strange because it was just Ben's reality and always had been. "My dad owns Walker Beach Construction. Froggies is my Uncle Thomas's. Aunt Kiki owns the antique store on Main. And Aunt Louise runs a shop that sells fancy oils and vinegars."

He nearly gagged as the words tumbled out. Since when did he tell strangers his family history? Ben stuffed the rest of his slice into his mouth.

"Oil Me This, right? I stopped in there and bought some smoky bacon olive oil."

"Mmhmm." He swallowed. How could he end their conversation without seeming rude?

Bella stood and walked to one of the old brown bookcases flanking the fireplace then squatted next to a stack of board games. "And did I see that the beach and that large community park on the water are named after your family?"

Maybe one-word answers would kill her inquiries. "Yeah."

She glanced back at him, eyes wide. "Is the entire town run by the Baker clan?"

"We were just one of the founding families." The way her mouth hung open was kind of comical. Ben couldn't help but chuckle. "OK, the biggest founding family. I have eleven first cousins on the Baker side, and that doesn't even include all of the cousins on my great-aunt's side—the Griffins. Almost all of them live in town."

"That's intense." Bella pulled a red box from the bookcase. "Where does this inn come in? Is it part of the Baker family legacy too?" She wandered back to the couches and sat with Yahtzee in her hands. What did she plan to do with that? Didn't she know the game required more than one player?

He scratched behind his ear. "My great-great-grandparents originally built the inn."

"That must be nice—to be part of something bigger than yourself." Bella's voice was almost wistful as she cleared a spot on the coffee table then opened the lid of the box. She placed two pads of paper, pens, a plastic cup, and five dice on the table.

Guess he'd been wrong about her not knowing anyone here. Bella was expecting company.

Instead of relief, a hollow ache pinched Ben's chest.

What was he *doing*? He couldn't afford to get distracted by a pretty face. Not again. The inn was too important, and he'd already allowed his grief to overshadow his responsibilities for the last seven months.

Here, at least, was a clear chance for him to escape. Ben cleared his throat. "I guess. It's a lot of work. And I probably should get back to it."

Bella eyed him. "You up for a game first?"

"Oh. I—"

"Unless you're afraid to lose. This was my favorite game when I was a kid, and I warn you—I am good." She smiled in challenge. The gesture softened the edges of her businesslike aura, making her a bit more . . . approachable.

Definitely more beautiful, if that were possible.

Danger, danger, Will Robinson. "I really shouldn't."

"Right. Sorry. I don't want to stop you from doing your work. Believe me, I understand having a busy schedule." Bella worried her lip and there— another flash of the vulnerability he'd glimpsed earlier in her eyes.

Was she playing him? Trying to manipulate him? Or actually disappointed he wasn't staying? Ben couldn't trust himself to tell anymore.

Curse you, Elena.

Probably he should give Bella the benefit of the doubt. At the very least, he should be a gracious host.

"No, no. I'd love to play." Fine, *love to* was a reach. A big one.

"You sure? Really, I don't want to keep you." The sincerity in her tone rang true. At least, he thought so.

He groaned inwardly at the seesaw in his mind. "I'm sure."

"Awesome. You know the rules?"

"Yep."

Bella placed the dice in the cup and held it out toward him.

"Ladies first."

A hint of another smile graced her lips before she shook the cup then tipped it. Dice spilled onto the table. Gathering three of them, she dropped the dice into the cup and rolled again. "I can't help noticing that you don't sound too happy about owning the inn."

Was she a mind reader? Or maybe a lawyer. That would explain the fancy getup from earlier and her ability to trick him into spilling his guts. "No. It's great. Just a lot of pressure." Pressure he was caving under.

Bella recorded her play on her paper pad and passed him the cup of dice. "So why not sell?"

He scoffed at her casual question. "Yeah, right."

"Why not?"

Ben shook and rolled the dice, snagging three fours, a six, and a one. He collected the last two and rerolled them. "My family has owned the inn for just about a hundred years. They built it from the ground up. I couldn't sell it even if I wanted to."

And some days, he did. He'd never planned to inherit it, had always figured he'd keep working for his dad's construction company like he'd been doing since he was sixteen. Maybe, eventually, partner with him.

But seven months ago Grandpa died, and Grandma signed over the inn to her eldest grand-child. She'd said it was too much for her "old bones" and that maybe he could infuse new life into the place.

And here he was, leading it toward an early grave.

He knew Grandma had probably just pitied him, was trying to give him something to focus on instead of how he'd been embarrassed and betrayed in front of the entire town two months before that. But he hadn't had the heart to tell her he wasn't ready to own a business, especially one he knew next to nothing about.

Bella glanced at his dice. "Four fours. Nice!" Then she looked back at him and shrugged. "Surely your family would understand. It's your life, after all." Her eyes caught his, and for a moment his insides buzzed around the edges—a foreign feeling he couldn't quite define. "This is a beautiful property. You must have received offers at some point."

He picked up the final dice, tossed it into the cup. It rattled around inside. "A few."

"Did you consider them?"

He let the dice fly across the table, hoping to see a four. Wouldn't he end the game by rolling a Yahtzee? It had been a while since he'd played.

A three stared up at him. So close.

Ben sighed. "For about a minute. But I can't in good faith sell. It's not just about me."

"What do you mean?"

"Look, this is Walker Beach. My home. I've lived here my entire life. Unlike the two idiots who used to own the properties on either side of me, I'm not selling to some money-grubbing real estate developer whose main goal is to ruin my town."

Bella flinched. And for good reason—he'd practically shouted the words. Oops.

"How would selling your inn ruin the town?" Bella collected the dice off the table. "It's not like you're running a vibrant business that's contributing massively to the economy."

Wow. "Way to shoot a guy in the heart."

Bella fumbled the dice onto the floor. "Sorry." She grimaced. "I shouldn't have said that. This place, its history, means a lot to you."

"It does." And a city girl like her couldn't possibly get it. "If I sell to the highest bidder, what is a peaceful vacation destination will become overrun with tourists who don't appreciate what makes Walker Beach special."

"And what is that?" She straightened in her seat.

"We're an artsy community with some unique shops and restaurants, but it's more than that." He really shouldn't have to justify himself to this stranger. But for some inexplicable reason, he wanted her to understand. "I guess, for me, it's just . . . everyone here is family, whether you're related or not. Folks care about each other and help each other. You can't find that in the big city or even in every small town you visit."

Bella leaned forward, hands folded over her stomach, wincing. Once again, he'd let his forceful tone loose. Some gracious host he was turning out to be.

"Sorry. You hit on a sore subject."

Without either of them officially ending the game, Bella began to put it away. "No, I'm sorry. I didn't mean . . . didn't realize . . ." She looked up at him, cheeks red.

Great. He'd embarrassed her. "It's fine."

"It's not." The game packed, she closed the pizza box and stood. "Thanks for the pizza and the game, but I'll leave you in peace now. Good night, Ben."

Then she turned on her heel and was gone.

Lying back on the couch, he rubbed his face and stared at the stark white popcorn ceiling. Peace? Ha. It seemed like Ben would never find peace again.

Guys failing miserably were bound to live in turmoil.

Fall in love with Ben, Bella, and the entire town of Walker Beach in All of You, Always, Book 1 in the Walker Beach Romance series, available today on your favorite ebook platform.

OR

Save yourself a little money by picking up the Walker Beach Box Set, which includes all four Walker Beach Romance novels PLUS an exclusive prequel novella only available with the box set purchase.

BOOKS BY LINDSAY HARREL

The Barefoot Sisterhood Series

The Inn at Walker Beach

Walker Beach Series

All At Once (exclusively available in the Walker Beach
box set)

All of You, Always

All Because of You

All I've Waited For

All You Need Is Love

Port Willis Series

The Secrets of Paper and Ink

Like a Winter Snow

Like a Christmas Dream

Like a Silver Bell

Like a Holiday Inn

Standalones

The Joy of Falling

The Heart Between Us

One More Song to Sing

Lindsay Harrel is a lifelong book nerd who lives in Arizona with her young family and two golden retrievers in serious need of training. When she's not writing or chasing after her children, Lindsay enjoys making a fool of herself at Zumba, curling up with anything by Jane Austen, and savoring sour candy one piece at a time.

She also writes sweet romantic comedies (same sweetness, same heat level!) under the pen name Kristin Canary. Check out her books there at kristincanary.com.

www.ingramcontent.com/pod-product-compliance
Lightning Source LLC
Chambersburg PA
CBHW061530310726
48972CB00008B/2395